The Desperate Hours

A PLAY

by Joseph Hayes

Based on the novel by the same author.

SAMUEL FRENCH, INc.

25 West 45th Street   NEW YORK 36

7623 Sunset Boulevard   HOLLYWOOD 46

LONDON   *TORONTO*

THE DESPERATE HOURS

For Marrijane

THE DESPERATE HOURS was first presented by Howard Erskine and Joseph Hayes at the Ethel Barrymore Theatre, New York City, on February 10, 1955, with the following cast:

(IN ORDER OF APPEARANCE)

(11 males; 3 females)

TOM WINSTON	*Judson Pratt*
JESSE BARD	*James Gregory*
HARRY CARSON	*Kendall Clark*
ELEANOR HILLIARD	*Nancy Coleman*
RALPHIE HILLIARD	*Malcolm Brodrick*
DAN HILLIARD	*Karl Malden*
CINDY HILLIARD	*Patricia Peardon*
GLENN GRIFFIN	*Paul Newman*
HANK GRIFFIN	*George Grizzard*
ROBISH	*George Mathews*
CHUCK WRIGHT	*Fred Eisley*
MR. PATTERSON	*Wyrley Birch*
LT. CARL FREDERICKS	*Rusty Lane*
MISS SWIFT	*Mary Orr*

Setting and lighting by Howard Bay
Staged by Robert Montgomery

Costumes by Robert Randolph
TIME: *The present.*

SCENE: *The City of Indianapolis.*

ACT ONE
A day in autumn.

ACT TWO
Later.

ACT THREE
Later.

NOTE ON THIS VERSION

For those who wish to reproduce the New York set, consisting of two levels, manuscripts of the play with floor-plans are available.

The version of the play in this book simplifies the entire production; certain small changes in dialog, although not in content or character, have been made to accommodate the play to an average stage.

Those producing groups which have them available might wish to elaborate somewhat on the setting suggested here by the use of overhead sliding black curtains instead of traveler curtains or by the use of wagon-stages or revolving stages. *The present version does not require any of this for an effective production.*

All of the space and props and furnishings described in the following pages can conveniently be accommodated on a stage measuring 30 by 16 feet, or less.

The lighting can be as simple or as complicated as an individual director wish to make it. In the New York production, all lighting was "realistic"—that is, whenever a light changed, it was because an actor on the stage turned a light on or off. However, this is not at all necessary. Certain scenes are, naturally, more effective if played in dimness, but the play can be done with full lighting at all times.

It is important that a director be aware—and that he make all actors aware at all times—that in those scenes in which a character is not involved in the action the actor should remain *absolutely motionless*. Because of the nature of the staging, any action whatever by an actor not involved directly in a scene that is being played will detract from the effect of that scene. *This is vital.*

For purposes of defining separate areas, it would be advantageous for the floor of the Sheriff's office to be raised a few inches above floor of house, or vice-versa, although this is not necessary. Also, if the porch area could be a step higher or lower than the living room floor, it would be helpful. In any event, all that is necessary is that the hall and master bedroom be lifted some inches above living room floor-level, two or three feet if possible.

SCENE

Then action throughout alternates between two sets on stage. In the first two acts the Hilliard home is at stage-right and the Sheriff's office is at stage-left. In the final act, the Hilliard home remains at stage-right and a corner of an attic room is substituted for the Sheriff's office at stage-left. (See floor plan at back of book for exact simplified stage-setting.) The action shifts back and forth between the two sets by the use of blackouts and traveler curtains which mask the set that is not in focus. These operate simultaneously.

The portion of the Hilliard home that is in view consists of a section of front porch at extreme right, the living room, a hall and bedroom. The house is of the "split-level" type in design, and the hall and bedroom are lifted above the floor of the living room by one, two, or as many steps as the stage will accommodate. (It might be pointed out here that the higher above stage-level that the bedroom and hall are lifted, the better, as this section is upstage and the action should be visible at all times.) The downstage right wall of the living room is invisible, imaginary; for this reason, it is advisable, although not necessary, that either the porch or the living room floor be lifted above stage-level by a few inches. A low planter box along the porch side of this imaginary wall will help the illusion of separation between porch and living room, also. A door opens inward from the porch to living room. Downstage of this front door—in the imaginary wall at Right—is a window, perhaps only the frame of a big floor-to-ceiling window. Up of the front door is another door leading into the den. At extreme left a door leads from the living room into the dining room and the kitchen area of the house.

8

Upstage is a hall, reached from living room floor level by steps. The hall is separated from living room by a bannister running its length. At the extreme right end of this hall, a door leads into Cindy's bedroom. Another door, upstage, gives access to Ralphie's bedroom. The door at left end of hall leads into the master bedroom, which is a visible part of the set. A large portion of this room is out of view, but the acting area centers around one end of the bed. Because of sight lines created by the Sheriff's office set, the bed may occupy a large part of the available space. The director should establish the acting area—that is, the section of bedroom in which actors are plainly visible—and then move bed into position accordingly, staging all action on that end of the bed and in the area between bed and the right "wall" of bedroom. This right "wall" is also imaginary as is the downstage wall of bedroom proper, but the fact that the bedroom area is lifted above floor level of living room creates the illusion. (It is important that actors in the bedroom, when listening, or attempting to listen, to what transpires in the living room should go to the bedroom door and press against it, rather than attempt to listen through the imaginary "walls.")

In the Hilliard living-room—which is a pleasant and typical upper middle-class home—there is an easy-chair at right; a love seat upstage along the hall, facing down; a sofa, also facing down, at approximately center of living room, with a table at the left end of it; and another chair, facing down at an angle, up left, along the bedroom "wall." The house suggests neatness, pleasant living, and in the course of the play the havoc grows until at the end of the action it is a shambles. There are two telephones: one in living room on table left of left chair and one on hall table right of Ralphie's bedroom door.

Approximately four feet upstage and approximately one-third of the distance from stage left, there is a solid black panel which will help to create the illusion of "distance" between the Hilliard home and the Sheriff's office sets. The traveler curtains run on a line from this panel to the downstage corners of the total stage, gathering behind the proscenium at each side. It is important that furniture and props be aranged so that these curtains entirely mask the set that is not in focus. (See floor-plan.)

In the first two acts, the Sheriff's office is at stage left: a bare sort of room with a wall clock, a swivel chair at a desk, another chair, metal files, radio and intercom apparatus and telephone on desk. In the last act, this set becomes the attic of the Wallings' house. The only set-change involves substituting an attic-type window upstage for the "police-station" window of the first two acts. The "attic" effect will be accomplished by substituting attic "junk" as props and background for the Sheriff's office furniture.

Although the traveler curtains designate the line for furniture and props, it should be remembered that much of the action of a scene can be staged downstage of this line and of all furniture; thus, the actual playing-area in each set is considerably enlarged by a free use of the downstage space in both sets.

THE DESPERATE HOURS

ACT ONE

ACT ONE

SHERIFF'S OFFICE

(Traveler curtain masks Hilliard home.)

The curtain rises; morning light fades in on the Sheriff's office. WINSTON, *a deputy sheriff inclined to matter-of-fact laziness, sits at desk, speaking on the telephone. On the desk are an intercom, radio apparatus, sheafs of papers, and so forth. The wall-clock reads 8:10.*

WINSTON *(plaintively)*
   Baby . . . didn't I just tell you? I can't leave till Bard gets here. *(He listens.)* Listen, baby—this night shift gets my goat as much as it does yours. You think I wouldn't like to be in that nice warm bed?
   (There is a buzz from the intercom on the desk.)
   Hold it. *(He speaks into the intercom.)* Yeah, Dutch?

DUTCH'S VOICE
   Winston . . . Bard's going to want those Terre Haute reports right away.

WINSTON *(irascibly, into intercom)*
   What do you think I'm gonna do with 'em . . . eat 'em for breakfast? *(He flips off the intercom, returns to the phone.)* Hello, baby . . . *(Listens.)* Yeah, that's what I said, isn't it? In that nice warm bed with you. Who'd you think I . . . *(Listens.)* Okay, okay, baby . . . go back to sleep and wait for Papa. *(Hangs up, shakes head, pleased; speaks with gusto.)* Give me a jealous woman every time!

[BARD *enters.* WINSTON *is sleepy and glad to be relieved.*

13

BARD *takes off jacket, removes gun from shoulder-holster through the following. All very casual and commonplace at first.*

BARD *(as he enters)*
Morning, Tom.

WINSTON *(stretching)*
Well! About time.

BARD *(stows gun in drawer of file)*
Overslept. Sorry.

WINSTON *(rising slowly)*
You got a lovely excuse.

BARD
I'll tell her you think so. *(At desk, rifles reports.)* Quiet night?

WINSTON *(preparing to go, crosses to Left.)*
If kids'd stay out of cars and off motorcycles, we'd soon be out of jobs around here.

BARD *(studying a report)*
Not another burglary in Speedway City? *(Laughs.)* This guy's getting tiresome.

WINSTON
A real sex-nut, that one. Same old story . . . all he took was diamonds and women's panties. What the hell's the connection.

BARD
You figure it out, Tom. *(Then tensing . . . so that from now on the pace and tone change.)* What's this?

WINSTON *(yawns, looking over Bard's shoulder)*
Federal prison break . . . Terre Haute. None of our concern.

BARD
  When'd it come in?

WINSTON *(ready to leave)*
  Hours ago. The three of 'em busted out some time before
  dawn . . .

BARD *(sits at desk, snaps button on intercom)*
  Why didn't you call me?

WINSTON
  Call you? Why?

DUTCH'S VOICE
  Yes, Jesse?

BARD *(into intercom)*
  Dutch . . . get me Lieutenant Fredericks, State Police.

WINSTON
  Jesse . . . remember what your Irish wife threatened
  last time I routed you out of the nest . . .

BARD
  Terre Haute's only seventy miles away. They could've
  walked here by now!

FREDERICKS' VOICE *(on intercom—crisp, middle-aged, cynical)*
  I wondered when you'd start yipping, Bard.

BARD *(quickly)*
  Fredericks . . . anybody sitting on anything?

FREDERICKS' VOICE
  I'm sitting on just what you're sitting on, Deputy. Only
  mine ain't sweatin'.

BARD
  Griffin's woman . . . Helen Laski . . . any dope on
  her?

FREDERICKS' VOICE

Not a trace. Chicago . . . Cleveland . . . St. Louis. All we know is she was here in town three weeks ago.

BARD

Just don't let any cop touch her. She's the beacon'll lead us straight to . . .

FREDERICKS' VOICE

Bard . . . it's an FBI case anyway. The city police've ripped whole buildings apart. We got the highways blocked. We're working through all the dives . . .

BARD

If Glenn Griffin wants to come here, no roadblock's gonna stop him. And he's too sharp to hole up any place you'd think of looking.

FREDERICKS' VOICE

Look, lad . . . get that chip off your shoulder. (Shortly.) You want Griffin so bad, go get him!

[BARD *flips off the intercom.* WINSTON *reluctantly removes his coat.*

WINSTON

Glenn Griffin . . . is he the one you . . . ?

BARD (thoughtfully)

Yeah . . . he's the one. (Studying reports.) Glenn Griffin . . . his brother, Hank . . . and . . . who's this third one? Samuel Robish.

WINSTON

Life-termer. A three-time loser. And nasty. (As BARD *picks up the phone and dials,* WINSTON *returns his coat to the hanger.*) You're not going to get any sleep today, are you, Winston? No, I'm not going to get any sleep today. I'm going to sit on the teletype machine like a good little boy scout . . .

[BARD *smiles a bit as* WINSTON *exits. Then he speaks into the telephone in contrasting gentle tones.*

BARD

Hello, Katie. Did I wake you? . . . I've just had an idea . . . why don't you go over to my mother's for the day? *(Laughs—but the urgency comes through.)* Oh, stop groaning . . . how often do I ask you to let her talk your arm and leg off? . . . No, not this afternoon. Now! . . . And Katie . . . don't mention where you're going, huh? . . . To the neighbors, anyone . . . Good . . . Right away. Take a taxi . . . Sure, splurge.

[BARD *hangs up, sits thinking, with the smile fading.* WINSTON *enters, with* CARSON, *who is youthful, business-like, rather studious-looking.* WINSTON *places a teletype message on desk before Bard.*

WINSTON

It had to break, Jesse. *(Then with a touch of sarcasm as* BARD *reads.)* Oh—this is Mr. Carson, FBI.

BARD *(briskly)*

How are you? Look, it says they beat up a farmer south of the prison before daybreak. How come we're just getting it?

CARSON

They left him in his barn, out cold . . . ripped out his phone. He just staggered into a general store and reported his car stolen . . . *(With a touch of good-natured irony.)* How are you?

BARD

Have you put this on the air?

CARSON

Deputy, I've been in touch with Sheriff Masters by telephone.

BARD

I hope he's enjoying his extended vacation . . . he sure picked a fine time to leave me in charge here . . .

CARSON

The way I understand it, you know this Glenn Griffin fellow better than any police officer in the area. How about your taking over this section?

[*Pause. The whole weight falls on* BARD. *He accepts it . . . slowly. Then:*

BARD

Okay . . . Okay . . . Let's find that car! *(He goes into action—hands teletype to Winston.)* Tom, put this description on the air. Tell 'em to repeat it every half hour.

WINSTON *(protesting)*

We'll be flooded with calls. Every crackpot in five states . . .

BARD *(sitting at desk)*

We'll follow up every tip!

WINSTON *(to* CARSON—*groaning)*

I hope you know what you just did!

[WINSTON *exits.* CARSON *moves to desk and offers* BARD *a cigarette.*

CARSON

Any idea where they might dig in?

BARD *(shaking his head)*

All I know is . . . just as long's Glenn Griffin's running around free and safe—with that prison guard's .38 in his paw—well, it's not free or safe for anyone else. No decent people anywhere—whether they've ever . . . *(The lights begin to dim.)* heard of Glenn Griffin or not . . .

HILLIARD HOME

Lights rise slowly. We see a typical house in the suburbs: pleasant, comfortable, undistinguished. ELEANOR HILLIARD, *an attractive woman in her early forties, enters from the dining room. She carries Dan's hat and topcoat, which she places on upstage sofa, then moves to front door, opens it and looks out. The morning light outside is bright and cheerful. Not finding the morning paper, she closes the door as* RALPHIE *enters from dining room.* RALPHIE, *aged ten, is dressed for school and carries a half-empty glass of milk, which he stares at balefully as he sits in Left chair.* ELEANOR, *who is extremely neat, is arranging pillows on the downstage sofa.*

ELEANOR *(gently)*
Ralphie, you left your bike outside all night again.

RALPHIE *(as though this answers her)*
It didn't rain.

ELEANOR
Well, it's not going to rain today, either. But you're go-ing to put it in the garage before you go to school.

[DAN HILLIARD *enters from dining room and crosses to front door to look out. He is a typical, undistinguished but immediately likable man in his forties.*

DAN *(calling toward hall)*
Cindy! It's eight-thirty.

CINDY *(off, in her room)*
Can't a girl straighten her girdle in peace?

DAN *(surprised)*
Girdle? . . . Girdle! *(Goes to Eleanor at Right end of*

sofa.) Ellie, can a twenty-year-old child with a figure like
Cindy's . . .

ELEANOR *(smiling)*
It's a joke, Dan.

DAN
Oh. Thank the Lord. She has to have a solid hour for
primping and then she complains all the way downtown
because we don't live in the city limits.

RALPHIE
Ain't love disgusting?

ELEANOR
Don't say "ain't."

DAN *(to Ralphie—firmly as he steps to Left)*
Don't say "love," either. *(There is a thud of a newspaper
thrown against the front door. DAN whirls, steps swiftly
to the door. He and ELEANOR have a slight collision. She
moves downstage and he opens the door and goes off
across the porch.)* Hey! Hey!

ELEANOR *(teasing—as she moves up Center)*
Try holding your nose and gulping it, Ralphie.

RALPHIE
It tastes sour.

ELEANOR *(picking up her small pad and pencil from end
table)*
Yesterday it tasted like chalk.

   *[She sits in Right chair and starts making her shopping
   list. DAN returns, picks up the "Indianapolis Star" from
   porch and enters the room, closing the door.*

DAN *(a suggestion of grouchiness)*
Some day I'm going to catch up with that paper boy and
we're going to have a lawsuit on our hands.

ELEANOR
Dan, you have time for a second cup of coffee.

DAN *(glances at his watch and then up to hall as he crosses Left)*
In half a minute she'll come prancing down and start urging *me* to hurry.

[DAN *exits into the dining room.* RALPHIE *takes a long drink of the milk but cannot finish it.* CINDY *emerges from her room, crosses to steps. She is dressed for work.* CINDY *is nineteen and attractive.*

RALPHIE
If cows only knew how I hated 'em!

ELEANOR
What would they do?

CINDY *(to Eleanor—from steps)*
Where's Dad? What was he shouting at me?

ELEANOR
What does he shout every morning at eight-thirty?

CINDY
He shouts it's eight-thirty.

ELEANOR
You win the kewpie-doll.

[CINDY *moves swiftly toward the dining room as* DAN *appears in the door with a cup of coffee.*

CINDY *(to Dan as she swings past him)*
Say, you'd better hurry!

DAN *(looks after* CINDY, *then to* ELEANOR *as he sits on sofa)*
What'd I tell you?

[DAN *sets his cup of coffee on the end table and picks up the newspaper and reads.*

RALPHIE

Dad . . . Why did the moron lock his father in the re-frigerator?

DAN *(his attention on the newspaper)*

Ralphie, do I have to answer that one?

RALPHIE *(brightly)*

Because he liked cold pop! *(There is an escape of breath from* DAN *which might or might not pass for a laugh.)* Well, why don't you laugh?

DAN

I laughed. What do you want me to do . . . roll on the floor?

RALPHIE

You almost rolled on the floor last night when I told you why the moron ate dynamite.

ELEANOR *(shakes her head warningly but continues writing)*

Ralphie . . .

RALPHIE

My name is Ralph. R-a-l-p-h. There's no Y on the end of it. I looked up my birth certificate.

ELEANOR

Sorry.

[*Through the following,* RALPHIE *rises and, with glass in hand, moves to the upstage sofa to pick up his jacket and football; he rather elaborately manages to conceal the half-glass of milk on the floor out of sight in the process.*

RALPHIE

Big game after school today. Fourth grade versus fifth grade. *(Having achieved his purpose; with a sigh of relief.)* We'll slaughter 'em! *(Kisses Eleanor.)*

ELEANOR

'Bye, darling.

[DAN *leans back to be kissed, but* RALPHIE *only glances at him and goes to front door, where* DAN'S *voice stops him.*

DAN

Hey! Aren't you forgetting something?

RALPHIE *(embarrassed and uncertain)*

Oh. *(He then returns to Dan, going downstage of sofa, and* DAN *leans for a kiss; instead,* RALPHIE *extends his hand and shakes Dan's hand with grave formality.)* So long, Dad. I hope you have a very pleasant day at the office. *(He turns and goes to the dining-room door, leaving* DAN *staring after him; calls into dining room.)* So long, dream-witch. I hope Chuck Wright doesn't even notice your new dress. *(Crosses toward front door at Right.)*

CINDY *(appears in dining room door, with glass of orange juice in her hand)*

'Bye. Flunk geography, will you, pest?

RALPHIE *(as he goes out the front door)*

Mister Pest to you.

[CINDY *disappears again in dining room and* RALPHIE *exits Right.*

ELEANOR *(rises and calls after him—out front door)*

Ralphie! Your bicycle!

DAN

What do you suppose that was all about?

ELEANOR *(toying with her pad and pencil—as she closes front door)*

Our son Ralph . . . spelled R-a-l-p-h . . . considers

himself too old to kiss a man . . . that's you . . . good-
bye or good-night.

DAN *(covering his hurt)*
   Oh.

ELEANOR *(moves to upstage of sofa)*
   He said last night he hoped you'd understand.

DAN *(with an empty smile)*
   I was hoping maybe he just didn't like my shave-lotion.
   (As ELEANOR *unconsciously touches his hair.)* Ellie, what's
   happening to both of them lately? This . . . this young
   lawyer Cindy works for . . . she can't be serious, can
   she?

ELEANOR
   She hasn't confided in me, Dad . . . which could mean
   she is.

DAN
   She's only twenty years old!

ELEANOR
   I was nineteen.

DAN
   You had some sense.

ELEANOR
   Sure. I married you.

DAN *(as though he has proved a point)*
   Well, I didn't drive a Jaguar!

[CINDY *enters from the dining room, pulling on her coat.*

CINDY
   Chuck and I find his Jaguar a very comfortable little
   surrey. *(Crosses to front door.)* Come climb into my Ford

coupé, Dad . . . and don't whisper when I'm in the next room. It's not polite.

DAN *(as he rises and moves to get his coat and hat from up-stage sofa)*
Now she'll speed.

ELEANOR *(automatically)*
Careful now, Dan.

CINDY *(satirically—chidingly)*
Mother . . . you say that every morning of the world. What could possibly happen to a man in the personnel office of a department store? *(She exits, closing the door; moves downstage on porch; exits Right.)*

DAN *(pointing at closed door)*
That's what I mean! That's not Cindy. Those are Chuck Wright's ideas. Last night on the way home, she asked me point-blank if I didn't think I led a pretty dull life.

ELEANOR
What'd you say?

DAN *(firmly)*
I said I didn't like Chuck Wright, either.

[DAN *goes to the door, and* ELEANOR *follows him.*

ELEANOR
Dan . . . at Chuck's age . . . you were going to be another Richard Halliburton, remember? Climb the Matterhorn . . . swim at midnight in the Taj Mahal. My father threatened to throw you . . .

[*Outside,* CINDY *taps horn impatiently.*

DAN *(embarrassed)*
I'm going to be late. *(They kiss: casual, without meaning, habit.)* If you're going to use the car today, buy some gas first. *Before* you have to walk a mile for it this time.

[DAN *exits, follows* Cindy. ELEANOR *closes the door.* ELEANOR *leans against the door a second, utters an almost silent "Whew," crosses to table at Left end of sofa, places her shopping list on table and flips on a small portable— battery-type—radio which is on end table. Through the following action, a newscaster's voice fades in:* ELEANOR *moves to Right chair, fluffs cushions, then to sofa where she folds paper Dan has thrown there, straightens the cushions. At this point she starts up the stairs, but decides to change stations on radio, so steps to it, turns knob and music fades in.*

NEWSCASTER'S VOICE
. . . five-state alarm. Police authorities have requested all citizens to be on the lookout for a 1941 Dodge sedan . . . gray . . . mud-spattered . . . bearing Indiana license plates number HL6827 . . . that is HL6827. One of the convicts is wearing a pair of faded blue farmer's overalls which were . . .

[*At this point* ELEANOR *changes stations; music fades in and she moves up the steps and into the master bedroom, leaving door open. The music plays, low, through the following.* ELEANOR *begins to make the bed.* GLENN GRIFFIN *appears on porch, rings door chimes. He is in his mid-twenties and wears faded blue farmer's overalls. He is tall with—at the moment—a rather appealing boyish expression on his handsome face.* ELEANOR *sighs.*

ELEANOR
Wouldn't you know it . . . *(As she moves out of bedroom and down steps.)* Every time . . .

[GLENN *rings chimes again—insistently, glancing around behind once.* ELEANOR *quickens her steps and opens door.* GLENN *smiles.*

GLENN
Sorry to bother you, ma'am, but it looks like I lost my

way. Could you kindly direct me to the Bowden Dairy? I know it's somewhere in the neighborhood, but I must have the wrong . . .

[ROBISH *appears in dining room door. He is large, bull-like, slow, with a huge head sunk between two upthrust shoulders. He wears prison garb. The following action has a cold, machinelike precision about it.*

ELEANOR

Let me see. I've seen that sign . . . but there are no dairies very close. You see, this is a residential . . .
[ELEANOR *becomes conscious of Robish's presence. She breaks off and turns. In that moment* GLENN *whips out the gun, forces his way into the room, pushing* ELEANOR. *He slams the door and locks it, then moves to* ELEANOR, *who backs to Right end of sofa, holding sofa arm with her hands behind her back.*

GLENN

Take it easy, lady. *(As her mouth trembles open.)* Easy, I said. You scream, the kid owns that bike out there'll come home an' find you in a pool of blood. (GLENN *only nods to* ROBISH, *who stumps up the steps and through the following looks into Cindy's room, Ralphie's room, then enters the master bedroom and searches the closet at extreme Left.)* You there, Hank?

HANK *(speaking as he moves into the living room from the dining room)*
All clear out back. Lincoln in garage . . . almost new. Garage lock broken. (HANK GRIFFIN *is younger than Glenn, shorter, not so handsome, with a confused, hard but somehow rather sensitive face.)*

[ELEANOR *looks at* HANK, *who returns her stare boldly. A shudder goes through her. Through the following,* GLENN'S *swagger suggests a deep insecurity.* ROBISH *is examining and discarding various of Dan's clothes in the bedroom . . . creating havoc.* GLENN *steps to Eleanor.*

GLENN

I'll take the keys to the Lincoln now, lady . . .

ELEANOR

Keys . . . *(She is backed up, downstage of sofa. Conquering shudders as she moves toward downstage Center.)* Keys? . . .

GLENN

Lady, when I talk, you snap. Snap fast!

ELEANOR

Top of . . . top of refrigerator . . . I think . . . I always misplace the . . . *(As* GLENN *nods to* HANK, *who goes into dining room.)* Take it . . . you only want the car . . . take it and go . . .

GLENN *(shouts)*

What're you doin' in there, Robish—takin' a bath?

ROBISH

Nobody home but the missus.

[*He goes into hall, with Dan's clothes. SOUND of back door opening and closing.*

GLENN

I figured it. *(He examines the house . . . looks into the den.)* Good-lookin' family you got, lady. I seen 'em leavin'. *(As* ROBISH *descends.)* How many bedrooms up there, Robish?

ROBISH

Three. An' three complete cans, for Chrissake . . .

[*The SOUND of a car door being slammed startles* ELEANOR.

GLENN

Don't be so jumpy, lady. Only the kid brother takin' care
of the cars.

ROBISH *(holding up Dan's suit)*

Th' sonofabitch's got five suits up there. *(He tosses the
suit over the back of Left chair and goes into the dining
room.)*

GLENN

Class, all the way . . . *(To Eleanor.)* I guess you're
tumbling to the idea, ain't you, lady?

ELEANOR *(picks up her purse from sofa)*

You want money . . . here . . . take it . . . anything . . .

GLENN *(takes purse and dumps contents on sofa)*

Pretty. *(Holds up a locket.)* Gold? *(As* ELEANOR *nods
wordlessly, he slips it into his pocket.)* I got a gal with a
yen for gold a mile wide. *(Picks up the money.)* This all
the dough you got in the house?

ELEANOR *(with difficulty)*

Yes . . . yes . . . my husband always says . . . too
much cash in . . .

GLENN *(grins)*

Old man's right. Ain't ever safe to have too much cash
layin' around. *(He pockets the money.)* Gives people
ideas.

[ROBISH *returns, disgruntled.*

ROBISH *(to Glenn)*

My gut's growlin'.

GLENN

We heard it.

ROBISH *(to Eleanor)*
Missus, where you keep th' liquor?

ELEANOR *(backing away from him)*
We don't have . . . I don't think . . .

GLENN *(gesturing to den)*
Robish . . . park your butt'n there'n keep your eyes
peeled that side-a th' house.

ROBISH *(aggressively; to Eleanor)*
I ain't had me a drink'n eighteen years.

GLENN
Robish, you don't hear so good. It's a kinda library. Im-
prove your mind.

[HANK *enters from dining room, crosses up Left corner
of sofa.*

HANK
Gray job's in the garage, outta sight. Lincoln's ready in
the driveway . . . headin' out. But she's low on gas.

[*He hands the car keys to* GLENN, *who pockets them.*
ELEANOR *moves uncertainly to Right chair, sinks into it.*

ROBISH *(stolidly)*
I need me a gun. (GLENN *nods to* HANK, *who turns and
runs up steps. Through the following, he looks into Cindy's room, Ralphie's room, and enters the master bedroom, where he searches through the closet extreme Left.)*
I don't like none of it.

GLENN *(moves to steps, calls)*
Hey, Hank, Robish don't like it. After them hard bunks
. . . them concrete floors!

HANK
Tell 'im to lump it.

GLENN

Lump it, Robish. *(Gestures to den.)* In there.

ROBISH

I don't feel right without a gun.

GLENN

Tell you what, Robish . . . let's you'n me go out an' stick up a hardware store!

ROBISH *(to up Center)*
Now you're talkin'!

GLENN *(sardonically)*

Sure . . . Come'n, Robish. Every copper'n the state's waitin' for us to pull a job like that! *(Moves to door.)* What're you stallin' for? (HANK *finds an automatic in the closet, pockets it and starts out of bedroom.)* Come on!

ROBISH *(turning away—growling, inwardly seething)*

Awwww . . . don't do me no favors. *(For the first time,* GLENN *laughs.* HANK, *on steps, watching Robish, joins in.* ELEANOR *stares.* ROBISH'S *face hardens and, scowling, he makes a sudden movement toward Hank.)* What're yuh yakkin' at, yuh . . .

[*But* GLENN *moves. The laughter dies. He grabs* ROBISH, *whips him about.*

GLENN *(in low hard tones)*

Lissen! How many times I gotta tell you? Keep your mitts off the kid, you don't wanna get your skull laid open. *(Pause.* ROBISH *and* GLENN *face each other. Then* ROBISH *turns sullenly and grabs suit of clothes from Left chair, growling.* GLENN, *having asserted his total control, laughs, takes cigar from humidor on end table and tosses it to Robish.)* Here . . . make yourself sick on a good cigar. (ROBISH, *seething, doesn't attempt to catch it; it falls to the floor. Then, defiantly,* ROBISH *steps on it, grinding it into the carpet.)* Robish, you gonna give the lady the idea we ain't neat.

ROBISH *(he picks up the humidor)*
Coupla brothers! Shoulda knowed better. Ain't neither one dry back-a the ears yet.

[ROBISH *crosses down of sofa and exits into the den.*

ELEANOR *(who has been watching in horror)*
What . . . what do you . . . ?

GLENN *(ignoring her, crosses to Hank)*
What'd you find? (HANK, *keeping his eyes on Eleanor, takes the automatic out of his pocket and hands it to* GLENN, *who examines it.* GLENN *turns to Eleanor.)* Lady, now I ask you . . . is that a nice thing to keep aroun' the house? *(He hands the automatic to Hank, whispering.)* Put it in your pocket and keep it there. Family secret, huh? What Robish don't know, don't hurt nobody . . . okay? (GLENN *laughs, gives Hank a playful push and throws himself onto sofa—in high spirits.)* Let 'em comb the dives!

HANK *(sits in Left chair; jubilantly)*
You foxed 'em good, Glenn.

GLENN
Came aroun' their roadblocks like we was flyin' a airplane! Everythin's chimin'! *(He becomes conscious of the comfort. He raises himself by the arms and sinks again into the sofa, delighted.)* Foam rubber, I betcha. Foam rubber, lady? (ELEANOR *nods.)* I seen the ads. *(He squirms in the seat, enjoying it.)* Melts right into your tail!

HANK *(rises, takes a cigarette from the box on the coffee*

table, lights it with the table lighter and hands it to
GLENN)
Christ, what a place to take the stir-taste outta your
mouth! Freezer full-a meat! Carpet makes you want to
take your shoes off!

ELEANOR
How long do you intend to . . .

GLENN *(casually)*
Be outta here by midnight, lady.

HANK
Midnight? I thought you said Helen was waiting . . .

GLENN
Not in town, Hank. We don't make it so easy for 'em.
She left three weeks ago.

HANK *(laughs, grabs a fistful of cigarettes from the box on
the coffee table, picks up the lighter, shoves it into his
pocket, picks up portable radio)*
I don't care if we never leave.

[*He exits into the dining room, carrying radio.*

GLENN *(rises)*
Now, lady . . . you think you can talk on the phone
without bustin' into tears?

ELEANOR *(rises with great difficulty, takes a feeble step, then
gets control of herself, straightens, and walks with dignity
and determination to the phone table at Left, turns to
face Glenn)*
Whom do you want me to call?

[GLENN *laughs as he crosses close to Eleanor.*

GLENN
I always go for a gal with guts! That's *whom* we're gonna
call—a gal with real guts. Person to person . . . Mr.

James calling Mrs. James . . . Atlantic 6-3389 . . . in
Pittsburgh. Pittsburgh, PA.

(BLACKOUT)

SHERIFF'S OFFICE

Lights rise swiftly. CARSON *sits in chair down Left, writing
on small note-pad. The clock reads 5:32.* BARD *is finishing a
telephone conversation, a note of exultation in his voice.*

BARD *(into phone)*
Yeah . . . okay . . . good deal! *(He replaces phone.)*
Pittsburgh! They've located Helen Laski. Avalon Hotel,
Pittsburgh. We'll have a record of any calls to or from
. . . in a few minutes now.

CARSON
Bard . . . stop me if I'm out of line . . . but what's
this thing to you? You, personally?

BARD *(slowly rubbing his chin)*
You've heard of that first law of the jungle . . . haven't
you, Carson? *(The light on the radio flashes.* BARD
presses the button, snaps) Deputy Bard!

WINSTON'S VOICE
Jess . . . this is Winston. Car three.

BARD
What've you got, Tom?

WINSTON'S VOICE
That hardware store holdup on the south side . . .

BARD *(eagerly)*
Yeah? Yeah?

WINSTON'S VOICE *(wearily)*
No guns stolen. All they took was fishing rods.

[BARD *presses the button and looks at Carson.*

CARSON
They'd be too shrewd to pull a stunt like that.

BARD *(steps toward Carson)*
Look, Carson . . . do me a favor. It's almost time for supper. All I've heard since morning is how damn wise those rats are. I'm up to here with it.

CARSON
Where're they getting their clothes?

BARD
My theory is they're running around naked so nobody'll notice 'em. *(The telephone rings.* BARD *picks it up.)* Deputy Bard . . . Yeah . . . *(Disappointment.)* Yeah. Okay. *(Hangs up.)* Helen Laski checked out of the Avalon Hotel last night. No phone calls, no messages of any kind received today . . . *(His eyes meet Carson's;* CARSON *shrugs.* BARD *bursts out.)* I know! I know! They'd be too smart to make a call to a hotel. They used somebody in between!

CARSON
I didn't say a word.

BARD *(moving downstage, grim)*
You know where that leaves us, don't you? Beating our tails ragged over nothing around here.

CARSON
Only you don't believe it.

BARD
Sure I believe it. I'm a trained police officer. I go by the facts, not crazy hunches. I reckon they're not here.

CARSON *(rises)*

Why don't you put some more patrol cars on the streets, anyway? Just in case?

BARD *(pacing)*

That damn jalopy's been reported in every state in the union . . . sixty times in Indiana alone! The earth won't open up and swallow it! Okay, let's try anything! *(He picks up phone, dials . . . as the LIGHTS DIM.) Where is that beat-up gray car?*

HILLIARD HOME

It is dark outside and dim throughout the house, except for the living room which is brilliantly lighted. ELEANOR *sits on the sofa, staring ahead.*

SOUND—music from radio in dining room: a loud jazzy tune—in contrast to the soft gentleness of the morning music.

The ravages of the afternoon are everywhere apparent; the atmosphere of invasion hangs over the entire house. There is an open box of cigars on the end table with some of the cigars scattered on the table. There is a carton of cigarettes, with the top ripped back, on the table. A coffee cup is also on the table and another is on the floor beside the armchair at Left. There are odds and ends of food. The ashtrays are filled to overflowing.

GLENN *is in Right chair, looking out window; he is filled with a sesne of triumph; he is almost gay, and his enjoyment of what follows is clear.* GLENN *wears a pair of Dan's slacks and a sport shirt.* ELEANOR, *alert in every fiber, is pale, haggard, stiff, sitting on chair at Left.* ROBISH *is entering from the den; he is wearing a full suit including shirt and tie— Dan's best, and it does not quite fit. A cigar is jammed in the corner of his mouth.*

ROBISH
What if this joker gets suspicious . . . that gray car parked right in his own garage?

GLENN *(casually)*
Can it, Robish.

ROBISH *(to Eleanor—as he crosses to steps)*
Why ain't he here? You said quarter to six.

ELEANOR
The traffic may be heavy . . . or Cindy may have had to work late . . . or . . . anything . . . anything!

HANK'S VOICE *(from dining room)*
Glenn! Black coop just turned in the driveway.

GLENN
Turn off the clatter back there, Hank.

[*SOUND: Radio turned off.*

HANK'S VOICE
You want me to grab 'em?

GLENN *(taking position facing front door—gun ready)*
Not with all them cars goin' by out there.

HANK'S VOICE
Woman comin' around to the front door, Glenn.

[ELEANOR *places her hand at her mouth.* GLENN *unlocks the door.)*

GLENN *(to Eleanor as he crosses to her)*
You don't have to do nothin' but keep your trap shut. *(He turns the gun to cover the front door.* CINDY *appears down Right and crosses porch to front door, enters, casually, swiftly, a trifle breathless. She stops dead when she sees Glenn.)* Come right in, redhead. (CINDY *backs away, pulling the door closed, but she suddenly stops,*

frozen in the door. The reason she stops is simply that GLENN *has turned the gun toward Eleanor's head.)* We still got the old lady, Sis. (ROBISH *is standing on steps, dull, brutish . . . with his little eyes roving over Cindy.* CINDY *closes the door and stands in front of it.* GLENN *grins.)* That's bein' real sensible.

CINDY *(planting her feet slightly)*
Mother . . . how long have these animals been here?

[ELEANOR *starts, as though she would warn Cindy.* GLENN'S *grin flickers, fades and a hardness comes into his face . . . but not into his tone.*

GLENN
Spitfire, too. You watch out, redhead.

HANK'S VOICE
Glenn! He's lookin' in the garage.

GLENN *(calling to Hank—confident, knowing)*
He'll come in. *(He grabs Cindy and pushes her toward Right chair.)* Sit down now, sweetie . . . and no talking. Not a goddam word.

HANK *(in pantry)*
He's coming around now—fast.

[GLENN *moves into position near front door. Pause. Then the door opens, and* DAN *enters, evening paper in hand.*

DAN
Ellie, whose car is that in the . . .

[GLENN *slams door shut behind Dan, and* DAN *breaks off, staring in bewilderment at Glenn, then at the gun.*

GLENN *(in flat cold tones)*
It's loaded. Now lock the door . . . *(Sardonically.)* Please.

[*Unable to speak yet, his eyes on Glenn,* DAN *turns and locks the door. Then:*

DAN *(baffled; softly)*
    What're you . . . why . . . I don't . . .

GLENN
    You never know what's comin', do you, Pop?

[DAN *then glances across to Eleanor.*

DAN
    Ellie? . . .

ELEANOR
    I'm all right, Dan.

DAN *(looking about the room, glances toward stairs)*
    Where's Ralphie?

ELEANOR
    Not home yet.

HANK'S VOICE
    Driveway ain't blocked, Glenn.

CINDY
    The house is crawling with them, Dad.

GLENN *(sizing her up)*
    Don't get me jumpy, redhead, this thing's liable to explode.

DAN *(flatly, glancing at newspaper in his hand)*
    Glenn Griffin.

GLENN *(laughs, takes paper)*
    Lotsa people heard-a me, didn't they? *(In satisfaction.)* Front page. *(Disgusted.)* They always gotta use the same goddam picture. *(He tosses the paper to the floor.)*

DAN

>Griffin . . . you fire that thing . . . and you'll have the whole neighborhood in here in two minutes.

GLENN

>I don't want to take that chance, Hilliard . . . any more'n you want me to.

ROBISH

>You dumb, mister?

GLENN *(Sizing up Dan)*

>Naw, he ain't dumb, Robish. He's a smart-eyed bastard, this guy . . .

DAN

>What're you . . . I don't understand . . . what do you want?

GLENN

>Take it easy, Pop.

DAN *(controlling himself with effort)*

>What do you want here?

GLENN *(takes a step toward Dan)*

>I don't want nobody to get hurt . . . What do *you* want, Pop?

DAN

>That's . . . what I want, too. *(Then, shrewdly.)* That's what you're depending on, isn't it?

GLENN

>You got it, Buster. First try.

DAN

>But . . . why here? Why my house?

GLENN

>Your break, Pop. I like the location. Those empty lots'n

both sides. The bike parked on the nice lawn. I like suckers with kids . . . they don't take no chances.

DAN

Anyone who could think up a scheme like that is . . .

GLENN *(cutting in)*
. . . is smart, Pop.

ELEANOR *(quickly)*
Dan! They've done nothing.

GLENN

Now I'm gonna explain the facts-a-life to you, Hilliard. You listen, too, redhead . . . listen good. You can get brave . . . any one of you . . . just about any time you feel up to it. Might even get away with it. *But* . . . that ain't sayin' what'll happen to the others . . . the old lady here . . . the redhead . . . the little guy owns the bike . . . *(Slight pause.)* Okay, Pop, you got it all the way now.

[*Another pause.* DAN *moves to sofa and drops his hat on it. Then he crosses, downstage of sofa, to Eleanor and turns to Glenn.*

DAN *(taking a deep breath)*
How long?

GLENN *(grinning—his eyes on Dan steadily)*
Now that's the kinda sensible talk a guy likes to hear.

DAN *(firmly)*
How long?

GLENN

Matter of hours . . . before midnight . . . maybe sooner. Meantime, everything goes on just like normal.

DAN

Why midnight?

GLENN *(almost politely)*
None-a your goddam business.

ELEANOR
They have a friend coming . . . with money.

DAN
What if . . .

GLENN *(speaking at the same time; stops Dan—steps toward Center)*
Lady, you speak when I tell you.

DAN
The police are looking everywhere for you. What if . . .

GLENN
They ain't looking here, Pop. They show here, it ain't gonna be pretty.

DAN
They could trail your friend . . .

GLENN
Let's get one thing straight, Pop. *(Gesturing to the window.)* Any red lights show out there . . . you folks get it first. *(There is a slight pause.* DAN *crosses to the window, going downstage of sofa, and looks out.* GLENN *laughs.)* Gives you a funny feelin', don't it? You don't know what's happenin' . . . or where . . . or what it adds up to . . . for you. Ever had that feelin' before, Pop? Me, I get it all the time. Even kinda like it. But you and me . . . we ain't much alike, are we, Pop?

CINDY *(a breath)*
Thank God.

DAN *(turns from window)*
Griffin . . . if you . . . what if I could get you the same amount of money you're waiting for? Now. Before midnight.

ROBISH *(steps down)*
  Hey, that don't sound like a bad . . .

GLENN *(moving to face Dan downstage of sofa)*
  Hilliard, you maybe think you're a big shot . . . fifteen
  thousand a year. But I had me a look at your bankbooks.
  Two hundred lousy bucks in the kitty. Hell, I had more'n
  fifteen grand in my hands at one time, Pop . . . and I
  ain't twenty-five yet.

CINDY
  I hope it helped pass your time in jail . . . counting it.

DAN
  I could raise more. I could . . .

ROBISH *(moves to upstage of sofa)*
  What about that? We could blow outta here right away!
  This joker's usin' his brain.

GLENN *(sharply)*
  Use yours, Robish. Helen's on her way *here.*

ROBISH
  To hell with that! Why should me and the kid risk our
  necks . . . just so you can get some copper knocked off!

GLENN *(dangerously now—low and intense)*
  Go spill your guts somewhere else!

ROBISH *(shouting)*
  What do I care who busted your goddam jawbone?

GLENN *(topping him—moves around Left end of sofa)*
  I'll bust yours if . . .

  [*They are now shouting at each other.*

ROBISH
  This guy talks sense. Don't I have nothin' to say? . . .

GLENN

NO! You ain't got a goddam stinkin' thing to say! (ROBISH *retreats slightly to up Right.* GLENN *turns on Dan more quietly but with force.*) You, Hilliard . . . I seen what you been up to. (*Crosses to Dan.*) Robish here, he ain't got a brain. But . . . he ain't got a gun, either. Don't try to get in between, you smart-eyed sonofabitch. Clickety-clickety-click. (*He makes a gesture at Dan's temple.*) I can see them wheels goin' around in there, Pop. Don't ever try that again! (*He backs away, eyes on Dan; speaks softly now—to Eleanor.*) Now, lady . . . serve us up that chicken you been thawin' out.

DAN

My wife's not your servant.

GLENN (*thinly . . . daring Dan to protest*)
I always wanted me a servant . . .

ELEANOR (*begins to rise*)
I don't mind, Dan.

DAN (*firmly*)
I do. Sit down, Ellie.

GLENN (*exploding wildly*)
Lissen, Hilliard! I . . . (*Then he stops; sizing Dan up, forcing control . . . almost quietly at first, building in intensity.*) I had a old man like you. Always callin' the tune. Outside his house, nobody. Inside, Mister God! Little punk went to church every Sunday . . . took it from everybody . . . licked their shoes . . . tried to beat it into Hank'n me . . . be a punk, be a nobody . . . take it from you shiny-shoed, down-your-noses sonsabitches with white handkerchiefs in your pockets! (*He snatches the handkerchief from Dan's breast pocket, spits into it, and throws it on the floor.*) You remember, Pop . . . I could kill you just for kicks. (*Pause. Without*

taking his eyes off Dan he against gestures to Eleanor, speaks coldly again.) Now, lady . . . get out there'n cook it.

[ELEANOR *starts to rise, but* HANK'S *voice stops her.*

HANK'S VOICE
Glenn! Kid comin' up the driveway . . . walkin' . . .

[GLENN *starts for the front door.*

DAN
Griffin . . . you've got to let me explain to Ralphie first . . .

GLENN
I don't got to do nothin'. You pull anything now, you can sit'n watch me kick the kid's face in.

HANK'S VOICE *(calling again)*
Comin' to the front door . . .

GLENN *(at front door, unlocks it)*
You got to learn to take orders from other people now, Pop . . .

[*The front door opens and* RALPHIE *enters, whistling.* GLENN *slams the door behind him and locks it.* RALPHIE *stops.*

RALPHIE *(bewildered)*
Hey . . . what is . . . (ROBISH *takes a single step.*) Who're you? *(He turns to front door, sees Glenn. A split second, then he runs to dining-room door . . . meets* HANK, *who emerges from dining room, stands in door.* HANK *now wears one of Dan's sweaters and carries the portable radio.)* Get out of . . .

[*Then* RALPHIE *whips about, as* DAN *reaches for him, and passes Dan downstage of sofa, running for front door.*

ROBISH *steps around Right end of sofa and cuts off Ralphie's escape downstage of sofa.*

DAN *(quickly)*
Ralphie, it's all right. Listen, it's . . .

[But RALPHIE *runs into* ROBISH, *who grabs the boy and shakes him roughly by the shoulders, venting on Ralphie the spleen that Glenn has stirred in him.*

ROBISH *(as he shakes Ralphie)*
Where ya think you're goin'? Don't you know who's boss aroun' here? Ya gotta take orders from Griffin! Griffin's the big shot aroun' here!

[As Ralphie's head snaps back and forth, DAN *moves in. He grabs Robish's arms and* ROBISH *releases* RALPHIE, *who dashes to* ELEANOR *at Left. She takes him in her arms.* CINDY *has stood up. She moves up of the sofa, to Left end.* DAN *slams Robish to Right, near window, and lets go with a blow that catches Robish on the side of the face.* DAN'S *mind has gone blank; he is propelled blindly by jungle atavistic forces beyond his control.* GLENN *leaps over the sofa as* ROBISH *roars and regains some balance.*

GLENN
It ain't gonna be like this! Not like this! (ELEANOR *stifles a scream as* GLENN *brings the gun down on Dan's shoulder from behind.* DAN *crumples onto the floor.* ROBISH *bends over him, his arm back for a blow, but* GLENN *sticks the gun in between, pointed at Robish.)* You hear me, Robish? *Nothin's gonna screw this up!*

ROBISH *(blinking owlishly at the gun in Glenn's hand)*
You think I'm gonna let that . . .

GLENN *(an order—low, intense)*
Get outta here!

ROBISH *(glaring. To Dan)*
OK, mister—I'll fix you. *(Crosses to dining room.)* My gut's growlin' again.

[ROBISH *kicks open the dining-room door and exits.* DAN, *his tie askew, manages to sit in Right chair, holding his shoulder.* GLENN *regains his familiar swagger.*

GLENN
Give the old lady a hand, redhead. Out there . . . if you please.

[CINDY *and* ELEANOR *rise,* ELEANOR *going into dining room, taking* RALPHIE *with her.*

CINDY
Where do we keep the rat poison?

[*As* CINDY *follows* ELEANOR, HANK *steps into her path, blocking her way, arrogantly.* GLENN *laughs and crosses so that* CINDY *is trapped between them.*

GLENN *(goading Dan)*
She's a honey, ain't she, Hank?

HANK *(arrogantly—as his eyes move over her)*
I don't go for redheads.

DAN *(sensing danger for Cindy)*
Griffin . . .

CINDY *(with a sharpness, to Hank)*
For God's small favors, make me eternally grateful.

[HANK *drops his arm and* CINDY *exits into the dining room.* HANK *follows her with his eyes and gives a low whistle.* GLENN *turns to Dan.*

GLENN
Kid's been in stir for three years, Pop. Don't cost nothin' to look.

DAN *(his eyes still on Hank)*
    Just don't try changing your mind, young fellow.

GLENN
    Hilliard, you're a funny gink. You don't know when you're
    licked, do you? . . . Now just one thing—you got a gun
    in the house?

    [*Slight pause.*

DAN *(carefully)*
    No . . . we don't.

GLENN *(enjoying himself)*
    That's right. You don't. Show him, Hank. *(After* HANK
    displays the automatic.) There for a minute I thought you
    was gonna lie to me, Pop.

    [GLENN *gestures for Hank to go to kitchen, and* HANK
    exits Left.

DAN
    Griffin . . . listen to me . . .

GLENN *(crossing to Dan)*
    I'll do the talkin'. You listen, Hilliard! That dough's half-
    way here now and nothin's gonna foul this up, see. You
    pull any of that muscle-stuff again . . .

    [*The following builds to climax.*

DAN
    That won't happen again . . .

GLENN
    . . . and I'm gonna let Robish work you over . . .

DAN
    . . . I went blank there for a . . .

GLENN

> . . . after that, you ain't gonna know what happens to the others. That the way you want it?

DAN

> Griffin . . . *(Very softly . . . with strength now.) hands off.*

GLENN

> I don't go for threats.

DAN

> Hands off, that's all I know! If one of you touches one of us again . . .

GLENN

> Don't talk tough to me, Hilliard . . .

DAN

> . . . I can't promise what'll happen . . . I can't promise *any*thing . . . if one of you touches one of us again. I don't *know* what I'll do. Can't you understand that, you half-baked squirt? I'll make you use that gun, Griffin. So help me. We're done for then, but so are you. *(Drops voice.)* It won't matter then whether your friend gets here or not . . .

(BLACKOUT)

SHERIFF'S OFFICE

The clock reads 7:03. WINSTON, *in Left chair, is trying to sleep. The radio signal is flickering.* BARD, *at desk, flips on radio.*

CARSON'S VOICE

> Bard . . . this is Carson.

BARD *(wearily)*
I'm still here, Carson.

CARSON'S VOICE
Helen Laski's been spotted.

BARD *(changing—alert and eager, excited)*
Where?

CARSON'S VOICE
She's heading west from Pittsburgh. On U.S. 40. Driving very slow and careful. Approaching Columbus, Ohio. Heading west!

BARD *(with satisfaction)*
West!

CARSON'S VOICE
Ought to be here about eleven or twelve tonight.

BARD *(an excited throb in his voice)*
Okay. Now listen. Don't let anyone tail her. I don't want her picked up, or alerted. But I want her clocked. Every town she goes through . . . every village. I want to know every time she stops to get gas, go to the can, anything.

CARSON'S VOICE
Looks like your hunch is paying off, Bard.

BARD
Could be, Carson. *Could be!* (BARD *flips off the radio, crosses to Winston.)* I told you they were homing pigeons, Tom! They do it every time . . . right back to the womb that spewed 'em.

WINSTON
Okay, they're pigeons. You're an owl. I'm sleepy. *(Pacing excitedly downstage.)*

BARD
They're layin' low here now . . . thinkin' how clever they

been . . . getting Laski out of town so she could back-
track to 'em. Clever! *Not so damned!*

WINSTON
Jess, you're raving. How long since you ate solid food?

DUTCH'S VOICE *(on intercom)*
Jess . . .

BARD *(flips intercom button)*
Yeah, Dutch?

DUTCH'S VOICE
Your wife called again. She says she's still at your
mother's but drowning in a sea of words . . . whatever
that means.

BARD *(with a laugh)*
Tell her to stay there all night, Dutch. Tell her I said it's
. . . uh . . . Be-Kind-to-Talkative-Mothers-Week. *(He
flips off the intercom, turns to Winston exultantly.)*
About twenty miles out of town, we'll put a real tag on
Miss Helen Laski and she'll breeze right in and lead us
straight to the hole! How many hours till midnight, Tom?

WINSTON
By my watch . . . *(The LIGHTS begin to dim.)* too
god-damned-many.

(BLACKOUT)

HILLIARD HOME

The living room lights are on; the bedroom in dimness.
GLENN *is in Right chair, slumped, legs stretched out.* ROBISH,
smoking a cigar, sits on steps. GLENN *is glancing out winodw.*
The family is arranged in a pattern: DAN *sitting on Right*
end of sofa, ELEANOR *beside him;* RALPHIE *stretched out on*

love-seat upstage, and CINDY *in chair to Left. . . .* DAN
glances at his watch.

GLENN
Pop, that's a good-looking timepiece you got there. *(He
extends his hand.)* I'll take it. (DAN *rises, pauses . . .
then slips the wrist-watch band off his wrist. He crosses
and hands the watch to* GLENN, *who examines it.)* Fancy.
(He slips it on his own wrist.) D'you snitch this from that
department store, Pop?

DAN *(quietly . . . with dignity)*
My wife gave it to me . . . on our twentieth anniversary.
(He returns to sit.)

GLENN *(winding the watch)*
Now ain't that real touchin'? *(To Ralphie.)* Hey, Buster
. . . . ain't it time for you to hit the sack? *(As* RALPHIE
rises and crosses to upstage of sofa.) You want to grow
up, be a big man like Pop here, don't you?

[RALPHIE *leans over, kisses Eleanor;* DAN *rises and moves
around Left end of sofa toward steps.* RALPHIE *then turns
and faces Glenn dierctly.*

RALPHIE
Mister . . . did anybody ever tell you? You *stink!*

[GLENN, *his face full of rage, reaches and grabs* RALPHIE
roughly; DAN *tenses. Then* GLENN *releases* RALPHIE *with
a short laugh.* RALPHIE *turns and starts toward steps, as*
ROBISH *rises, and* DAN *moves also toward steps.*

GLENN
Some brat you got there, Missus. Someday he's gonna get
his head knocked off.

ROBISH *(to Dan)*
What you think you're gonna do . . . go to the toilet for
him?

[DAN *glances at* GLENN, *who smiles.*

GLENN

It's his house, Robish. Hilliard don't want that kid hollerin' out a window any more'n we do.

[ROBISH *steps out of the way—toward Center.* DAN *and* RALPHIE *go up the steps.* DAN *opens doors of master bedroom and with his arm about the boy's shoulder, draws him into that bedroom.*

RALPHIE

How come?

DAN

I want you to sleep in here with us tonight.

[RALPHIE *sits on end of bed.* DAN, *abstracted, goes to window, looks out. In the living room,* GLENN *gestures to den.*

GLENN

Robish, get in there'n turn on the television.

ROBISH

There ain't no fights on—

GLENN

Jus' keep it lit up so's it looks normal from out front, that's all. . . .

[ROBISH *exits into den.* GLENN *turns off living-room lights, or he turns off one lamp, dimming the room.* NOTE: *It is not necessary that any lights be turned off or down in living room but it adds to the effect of the bedroom scene and what follows if the lighting is dimmed somewhat in living room.* GLENN *sits in chair to Right. In the bedroom,* RALPHIE *studies his father's back a moment before he speaks.*

RALPHIE

Dad . . . they're not so tough.

DAN *(still abstracted)*

Don't you fool yourself, Ralphie.

RALPHIE

You could've licked the big guy if that Griffin hadn't . . .

DAN *(turning to the boy)*

Ralphie, we can't lick them . . . at least not that way.
I lost my temper, that's all. I . . . can't let that happen
again.

RALPHIE *(not daring to believe it)*

Dad . . . are you scared?

DAN

Of course not. Why, you ought to know . . . *(He suddenly kneels on floor, facing the boy.)* Ralphie, listen to
me. Those two guns they have down there . . . they're
loaded. Those are real bullets. When a gun goes off, it
doesn't only make a sound. Those bullets can kill people.
Do you understand that, son?

RALPHIE

I've been thinking . . . I could climb out the window
of Cindy's room . . . out across the porch roof . . . I
could get to the Wallings next door. Get help . . .

DAN *(patience running thin)*

Ralphie . . .

RALPHIE

The porch isn't much higher'n the garage roof. I've
jumped off the garage roof a lot of times.

DAN

Ralphie, how many times have I told you to stay off the
garage roof?

RALPHIE
You could, though. I'll *bet* you could.

DAN
Look, Ralphie . . . Listen, Ralph . . . *Ralph.* You
want me to call you Ralph, don't you? You want to be
considered a grownup boy in this house? Then you've
got to behave like one . . . *think* like one . . . beginning right now!

RALPHIE
Is that why you want me to sleep in here—so I can't
climb out Cindy's window?

DAN *(anger rising)*
Ralphie, didn't you hear them? If you got out of here
. . . even if you brought the police . . . do you know
what would happen? They would shoot your mother and
your sister . . . and *you* . . . *you'd* be the reason they
did it.

RALPHIE
You *are* scared.

DAN
No, no, of course not . . . It's only . . . *(Suddenly
changes.)* Yes, son . . . yes, I'm scared. But I'm not
ashamed of being scared . . . Sometimes it's better to
be scared. You think about that now. You think hard
about that, hear?

RALPHIE
Well, I'm not. And Cindy's not either.

DAN *(rising, urgently)*
You're not to leave this room tonight, do you hear—

[*The telephone in the house rings.* DAN *stops. Immediate
tension . . . There is a pause until the second ring starts.*

GLENN *rises and turns on the living-room lights.* ROBISH *appears in the door of the den.*

GLENN

Hank! *(To* CINDY.) Okay, redhead . . . you get the pleasure. (CINDY *rises.* HANK *enters from dining room;* GLENN *gestures to other phone in hall.* HANK *goes up the steps to that phone.)* If it's for Mr. James, I'll take it. Anyone else, let 'em talk . . . except the brat.

[*The telephone continues to ring—insistently, mechanically.* HANK *picks up the phone in the hall with his hand on the circuit breaker in the cradle until he hears Cindy speak. Then he opens the circuit and listens.* DAN *stands at door of bedroom . . . alert, waiting.*

HANK *(when he is ready at the phone)*
Okay, Glenn.

GLENN *(beside Cindy at the phone table)*
Like any other night, see. Normal.

[CINDY *picks up the phone with her left hand.* GLENN *grabs the instrument and puts it in her right hand so he can try to listen, too.*

CINDY *(into phone)*
Hello? . . . Oh . . . No, I can't . . . not tonight . . . I simply can't, that's all . . . Nothing's the matter, I . . .

[*She slowly replaces the phone. In hall,* HANK *replaces the extension and faces the living room.* DAN *opens the door of Ralphie's room.*

GLENN *(to Cindy—impatiently)*
Well? *Well?*

CINDY *(bleakly)*
I flunked.

GLENN
> Who was it?

CINDY
> It was Anthony Eden.

HANK *(descending steps)*
> His name's Chuck. And he's coming, anyway. For a date.

> *[Pause . . . HANK'S eyes on Cindy. GLENN takes a few steps down Left, thinking furiously. DAN emerges from bedroom and closes door.*

GLENN
> You ain't 's wise's I thought you was, spitfire.

HANK
> She couldn't help it. He was in a drug store around the corner. Wouldn't even listen. Wants her to go dancing.

GLENN *(turns to Cindy)*
> Okay. You be ready, cutie. When Anthony Eden stops out front, you duck out . . .

> *[Pause: general amazement.*

ROBISH
> Griffin . . . you off your rocker?

GLENN *(calling)*
> Hilliard . . . come 'ere. *(To Eleanor.)* You stick with the brat, he don't get no ideas.

> *[ELEANOR rises and goes up the steps, passing DAN as he descends.*

DAN *(to Eleanor, in a low voice)*
> Lock the door.

> *[GLENN flips on portable radio on end table, then crosses to Cindy as the music rises.*

GLENN

You wanna dance, redhead? You should-a told Hank. *(Crosses to Hank)* C'mon, kid, you want a dance, take a dance. *(To* CINDY, *who moves slightly away to Left.)* Give the kid a break, spitfire.

[DAN *watches tensely . . . as* HANK *looks Cindy over, with arrogance, but the longing clear in his face. Then* HANK *moves, crossing, picks up radio, flips it off. In silence, he walks with dignity, inwardly disturbed, toward the dining-room door, exits. A moment—while* GLENN *stares after Hank, amazed, frowning. Above,* ELEANOR *enters bedroom, closes and locks door, turns off bedroom light, goes to window.*

GLENN *(baffled, almost to himself—looking at closed dining-room door)*

Oughta see Hank dance. Has all the babes groggy. *(Recovering, turning to Dan.)* Hilliard . . . the gas is low in that fancy buggy of yours. Fill'er up'n check the battery'n oil.

ROBISH

You ain't lettin' 'em *both* out?

GLENN *(crosses to Dan up Center)*

The kid'n the missus stay. Him or the redhead pull something, they know what'll happen here. Pop here's a smart cookie. He don't want no coppers settin' up machine guns on his nice smooth lawn . . . throwin' tear gas through his windows. *(Moves closer to Dan, threateningly.)* Cause that happens, you know who's gonna get it, don't you, Hilliard? Not you. *(He gestures upstairs.)* Them. I'm gonna see to it personal. *(Slowly.)* An' you're gonna stay alive to remember it the rest of your life.

[*There is a pause. Then* DAN *looks at Cindy.*

DAN

You hear that, Cindy?

[DAN *crosses to love-seat and gets his coat. In bedroom*
RALPHIE *stretches out on bed.*

CINDY

I'll do *anything* to get away from that voice.

ROBISH

Okay, everybody's gone nuts. Gimme some liquor.

DAN *(looking at Robish, then turning to Glenn)*
No, no liquor.

GLENN *(sits in Left chair)*
This time the old man's right, Robish.

ROBISH *(shrewdly—striking the weak spot)*
You lettin' this joker give the orders?

GLENN *(tricked)*
Nobody gives me orders. Not ever again! *(To Dan.)*
Make it bourbon, Pop. Bonded. *(To Cindy.)* You . . .
bring back some late-edition papers. *(He sits.)*

CINDY *(scathingly—as she crosses to love-seat to pick up
her coat)*
Would you like a scrapbook and a jar of paste?

HANK'S VOICE *(calling)*
Glenn! Car stoppin' at the curb. Little low-slung job.
Foreign make, some kind.

CINDY *(faces Glenn)*
It's a Jaguar. You should know what a jaguar is . . . it's
a fierce jungle animal . . . very brave against smaller,
less ferocious animals. But it's a snarling coward when
trapped.

[*She goes to the front door.* DAN *follows her, stops her.*

DAN

Cindy! *(She turns to him; slight pause; then gently.)*
You . . . you be careful, hear?

[*As* DAN *opens the door,* GLENN *rises quickly and flattens
himself against "wall" to Left of Left chair.* CINDY *goes
out and* DAN *closes the door.*

GLENN

If that spitfire tries anything!

DAN *(crosses to down Right corner of sofa)*
Griffin . . . what if the police track you down? Sooner
or later . . . through no fault of ours . . what if . . .

GLENN *(smugly—in control, as he moves to down Left
corner of sofa)*
I'd never know who done it, Pop.

DAN

But you couldn't blame *us!*

GLENN *(slowly)*
Hilliard, I got news for you. I—can—do—anything—I
want. Nice family you got here, Pop. You love that woman
of yours, you ain't gonna reach for no phone in that filling
station. Them coppers're after *me,* y'know. They don't
give a hoot in hell about you. *Or* your family. *(He crosses
to the front door.)* Clickety-clickety-click . . . give you
something to think about, Pop.

[GLENN *opens the door and gestures Dan to go.* DAN *goes
out, setting his shoulders. Above,* ELEANOR *watches out
bedroom window.*

ROBISH *(as* GLENN *closes and locks front door)*
Jeez, I'm gettin' up a thirst all of a sudden.

[ROBISH *exits into den.* GLENN *looks out "window" down
Right, watching* DAN *cross porch and disappear at extreme*

down Right. In a moment HANK *enters from dining-room.*
He looks quiet and moody as he moves toward Left chair.
GLENN *turns from window.*

GLENN

Kid, everythin's chimin'! Told you I'd shack you up in
style, didn't I?

HANK *(noncommital—as he sits)*

Yeah . .

GLENN *(crosses to Hank)*

Hey . . . what's eatin' you, anyway?

HANK

Y'know something, Glenn? I never had a "date" in my
life.

GLENN

Date? Hell, you laid enough babes to . . .

HANK

Naw, I mean a *date*. Y'know . . . ordinary things like
that.

GLENN *(scornfully)*

Malted milks? Hot dogs at a drive-in?

HANK

Maybe . . .

GLENN

You got it comin', kid . . . all the babes you can handle
and still walk straight up.

HANK

Babes like Helen?

GLENN *(astonished)*

Yeah . . . What's the matter with Helen?

HANK

> She's a tramp.

> [HANK *rises abruptly and goes to dining-room door, disappears.* GLENN *stares after him, puzzled.*

(BLACKOUT)

SHERIFF'S OFFICE

> BARD *is at the desk, working over various reports.* CARSON *enters briskly. Clock: 8:56.*

CARSON

> Bard . . . hold onto your hat. She's not coming.

BARD

> What're you talking about . . . not coming? She's halfway . . .

CARSON *(shaking his head—firmly)*

> Helen Laski's not coming. She make one simple mistake. She ran a red light on the outskirts of Columbus. A patrol car gave chase.

BARD *(rising, outraged)*

> Carson . . . are you telling me they arrested Helen Laski for a *traffic violation?* Good God, they had orders! It's been on every teletype for hours . . . *do not arrest!*

CARSON

> They didn't arrest her. She gave them the slip . . . in downtown Columbus. Abandoned the convertible. Swallowed up. Presto! *(He shrugs.)* These mistakes are bound to happen.

BARD

> You can't afford mistakes against a mind like Glenn Griffin's! *(He sits at the desk and flips the button on the intercom.)* Dutch! I want every long distance tele-

phone call and a record of every telegram from Columbus, Ohio, to Indianapolis from . . . *(He looks at Carson.)*

CARSON

Eight.

BARD

From eight o'clock to now . . . and straight through the night. As fast as they get 'em. Any number to any number. Names, addresses, the works. *(Flips off the intercom, moves down Left.)* Imagine those greedy sonsabitches in Columbus trying to pick her off for a lousy fifteen-buck fine! !

CARSON *(sits at desk, and picks up the deck of cards on the desk)*

She has to contact him . . . wherever he is. All we can do is wait. How about a game of double solitaire?

BARD *(pacing up Left; tensely)*

Wait . . . wait . . . wait.

(BLACKOUT)

HILLIARD HOME

In bedroom, ELEANOR is turning away from window. She moves to bedroom door. RALPHIE lies asleep on extreme Left end of bed. In living room GLENN is rising from his position at "window" down Right and ROBISH is entering from den.

ROBISH

Tired-awaitin'. I been thinkin' about a snort of whisky for eighteen years.

GLENN *(as he moves tensely to up Center)*

Shut up, he's comin' in. *(He gestures for ROBISH to unlock door.* ROBISH *unlocks and opens the front door.* DAN *enters, the fury and frustration packed solid through his whole frame. A new fear has taken root in him now, and he speaks flatly, quietly.* GLENN *says:)* C'mere, Pop. (DAN *crosses and* ROBISH *closes and locks the front door.)* You mind takin' your hands outta your pockets? (DAN *obliges.)* Thank you kindly . . .

ROBISH
Where the hell you been?

[DAN *faces* ROBISH. GLENN *frisks him expertly.*

DAN
The service stations close early in this neighborhood . . . (GLENN *is circling Dan.)* I don't have a gun, Griffin.

[GLENN *brings the whisky bottle out of Dan's coat pocket. It is in a paper bag which he removes and drops on the floor.*

ROBISH *(outraged, seeing the bottle)*
Chrissake, a pint!

DAN
You didn't specify any particular amount.

GLENN *(looking at the bottle—whistles appreciatively)*
Nothing but the best for Pop! *(As* ROBISH *snatches the bottle.)* Robish, go'n out'n check the car over. *(He sits on the sofa, putting his feet up.)*

ROBISH *(working with the bottle)*
Maybe he's got coppers stashed in the back seat. Let Hank check it.

GLENN *(dismissing it—lifts voice)*
Hank! Check the car.

HANK'S VOICE *(bitterly)*
Okay, Glenn.

[DAN *goes to the steps, begins to mount. SOUND: Back door closing.*

GLENN

You didn't get any ideas out there, did you, Hilliard?

ROBISH *(struggling with bottle at Right)*
Kee-rist . . . eighteen years an' then you can't get it open! *(Succeeds, takes a long swig from bottle.)*

DAN *(calls)*
Ellie . . . ?

ELEANOR *(opens bedroom door)*
We're all right, Dan. Cindy's not back yet.

GLENN

Pop, when I ask you a question, you answer!

DAN *(turns, flatly)*
No. No ideas.

[*Above,* ELEANOR *closes the door.*

HANK

Car's okay. *(He enters from dining-room door, pauses at Left.)* I didn't try the motor. *(A glance at Dan.)* Looks like the whole street's gone to sleep.

GLENN

See, Robish. Hank ain't yellow. Taught him how not to be yellow, didn't I, Hank?

HANK

You taught me everything.

[*The strange twist of bitterness in his tone causes* GLENN *to look at him sharply.*

DAN *(haunted by his new fear—steps to Left end of sofa)*
Griffin . . .

GLENN *(briskly; unpleasantly now)*
Your woman's waitin'. Go to bed.

DAN *(firmly)*
Griffin . . . when you do leave tonight, we're staying in this house. My family. All of us.

GLENN *(eyes on Hank—across Dan)*
Yeh, yeh. You give me a fair shake, I give you a fair shake.

[*Pause.* DAN *stands thinking a moment, then turns, goes to bedroom.* ELEANOR *comes to meet him as he enters.*

ELEANOR
Dan . . . did you?

DAN *(leaning back against door)*
I did just what they told me.

[ELEANOR *is relieved.* DAN *crosses to look out window. In the living room,* HANK *crosses to Right, takes bottle from Robish, drinks.* GLENN *goes to Hank, takes bottle, looks across it at Hank.*

GLENN
I did teach you everything, didn't I, Hank?

HANK *(as* GLENN *starts to take a drink)*
Yeh. *(Levelly.)* Everything. Except maybe how to live in a house like this.

GLENN *(lowers bottle in amazement, not drinking)*
Live here?

[ROBISH *takes bottle and* HANK *moves to slump in Right end of sofa.*

ROBISH *(drinking as he exits into den)*
Ahhh . . . my gut's beginnin' to burn good.

[GLENN *moves around Right end of sofa to face Hank;* GLENN *is baffled.*

GLENN *(baffled)*
Live here? We ain't gonna *live* here.

HANK
No. Or any place like it. Ever.

GLENN
Hank, what the hell's . . .

HANK
When Helen gets here, we gonna give Hilliard a fair shake?

GLENN *(angrily)*
Anybody ever give *you* a fair shake?

HANK
Who the hell ever had a chance?

GLENN *(an idea; his tone changes)*
The redhead! She got you goin', kid? *(Laughs and kneels facing Hank; with warm comradeship.)* Tell you what, kid . . . when we leave, we'll take her along. Just for you.

HANK *(after a pause—bitterly)*
Fair shake!

GLENN *(anger again)*
What you think I'm gonna do? *(Trying to sell Hank the idea.)* Nobody's gonna be suspicious if we got two women'n the car. We'll take 'em both. *(He gives Hank a playful punch.)* You give me the idea yourself!

[*In reply* HANK *rises and strides toward dining room, exits.* GLENN *is bewildered. He looks after him a moment; then he follows. Above, in bedroom,* DAN *turns from win-*

dow and faces ELEANOR, *who has remained leaning with her back against the door.*

DAN *(bitterly)*
I did just what they told me! *(Moves downstage.)* I saw the Wallings coming home from the movies. I could have . . . *(Bursting out rebelliously.)* What *should* I have done, Ellie?

ELEANOR
Nothing. If the police come, Dan . . . it could be worse.

DAN
And if they dont? . . . You can't deal with boys like that. With guns in their hands. Stone walls! If you could just *talk* to them . . . *reason* . . . be sure he means what he . . .

ELEANOR
Dan . . . it won't be long now . . .

DAN *(sits on end of bed)*
It makes no sense! You open a door . . . a door you've opened thousands of times . . . and wham, all of a sudden the whole world makes no sense!

ELEANOR *(moves to him, puts her hand on his shoulder)*
Dan, some day we'll look back on these hours and . . .

DAN *(quietly)*
Ellie, there is no *some day*. They've all been smashed now . . . *(He turns away.)* broken off . . .

ELEANOR
They can't do this to you! I won't allow them to . . .

DAN
My brain's like a stone in my head. All this must've started months ago . . . maybe years . . . when that kid down

there started hatching this scheme in his cell . . . before
we ever even heard his name . . .

ELEANOR

Dan, it's such a short, *short* time. Any minute now. All
they'll have is the car. Even that's insured . . . isn't it
silly, the things you think of? As soon as they've gone,
you'll pick up the phone . . .

[*The expression on* DAN'S *face stops her.*

DAN *(turning away—flatly)*
Just like that . . .

ELEANOR *(kneeling on floor, facing Dan)*
Dan . . . what are you thinking?

DAN

I'm thinking a man could be haunted forever . . . after-
wards . . . by the thought that if he'd done just this at
the right time . . . or that at just the proper moment
. . . he might have prevented it all.

ELEANOR

No, no, something else. When they leave you'll pick up
the phone and . . . *(Stops; realizing.)* They won't let
you do that, will they?

DAN *(rising; speaks reassuringly now)*
Of course they will, darling . . .

ELEANOR
No!

DAN
Shh . . .

ELEANOR
How can they stop it?

DAN *(takes her arms in his hands)*
They can't. There's no way to . . .

ELEANOR *(finally)*
I know, Dan. I *know!*

DAN
Don't imagine things, Ellie!

ELEANOR *(hollowly)*
They'll have to take someone along . . .

DAN
No, Ellie, no. The thought never occurred to me.

[RALPHIE *appears, sitting up on bed;* DAN *sees him as*
RALPHIE *moves on bed toward his parents.*

RALPHIE
Dad—

DAN *(whirling about)*
Hey . . . hey, skipper . . . I thought you were asleep.

RALPHIE *(to Dan, their eyes locked)*
Are you going to let them . . . what you just said . . . ?

DAN
Ralphie, I just explained to your mother . . .

ELEANOR *(moves upstage of bed to place her arms around
Ralphie's shoulders)*
Dear, your mother had a wild idea, that's all. Those men
haven't even thought of that.

RALPHIE
I don't want them to take me along with them.

DAN *(kneeling)*
I wouldn't let them do that, Ralphie. You ought to *know*
I wouldn't let them do that!

RALPHIE *(backs away, turns)*
How are you going to stop them?

[*Pause.* DAN *and* ELEANOR *look at each other, helplessly. The sound of an approaching motorcar is heard. There is immediate tension.* ELEANOR *steps to the window.* HANK *bursts in from the dining room, gun ready, moves carefully to the front "window" at Right. Car motor stops, off Right, and two car-doors slam.* CINDY *appears at extreme down Right, followed by* CHUCK, *who is a rather ordinary-appearing young man in his mid-twenties. He wears a sports-coat and an expression of bewilderment.* CINDY *starts along porch toward front door. Inside house,* HANK *is at Right chair, looking out "window," being careful to stay out of sight and to create the illusion, for audience, of a wall and window between living room and porch.*

CHUCK *(catching up with her)*
Cindy . . . are you going in like this?

CINDY
Please, Chuck!

CHUCK
Look, I know I bowled you over. I've bowled myself over, too. But when a fellah proposes to a girl, he kind of expects an answer . . . like yes or no . . . not: "Take me home, Chuck!"

CINDY *(her mind elsewhere)*
Was . . . was that a proposal?

CHUCK
Well, it wasn't much of one, but it was the best I could manage . . . with you off on another planet somewhere. I don't mind admitting you've got me so balled-up to-night, I . . . *(Shakes his head as* CINDY *fumbles in her pocket for her keys. He touches her arm.)* Look . . . redhead . . .

CINDY *(whirling on him; sharply)*
Don't call me that!

CHUCK
  But I always call you . . . All *right!* One minute you act
  like you hate me . . .

CINDY
  Oh, no . . .

CHUCK
  . . . and the next . . .

CINDY
  Chuck . . .

CHUCK *(hopefully)*
  Yes? . . .

CINDY
  Chuck . . . listen.

CHUCK
  Well? . . .

CINDY *(abruptly changing her mind)*
  I'll tell you tomorrow . . . at the office.

CHUCK
  You'll tell me one thing right now . . .

CINDY *(tensely, turns away)*
  It doesn't concern you, Chuck.

CHUCK *(turns her around, takes her hands)*
  If it concerns you, it concerns me. There. That's all I've
  been trying to say all evening. You've done something to
  me, Cindy. I've known a lot of girls . . . but . . . but
  you've opened doors . . . in me . . . in the world. So
  I've got to know . . . now . . . have I been kidding
  myself? Are you closing the doors? *(Suddenly,* CINDY
  *throws her arms around his neck and kisses him, indes-
  peration, deeply touched, clinging to him. He slips his
  arms around her waist. Inside,* HANK *is watching . . .*

turns away. They break the kiss slowly and CINDY *lays her head against his chest.)* Cindy . . . you're trembling all over. *(He lifts her chin.)* You'd better tell me.

CINDY

Yes . . .

CHUCK

Your family? . . . *(She nods.)* Cindy, you can't fret about it. If it's them. Because . . . look . . . it's *you. You're* the one I want to take care of now. *Only* you. *(She stares, realizing that she cannot tell him.)* Well, Cindy?

[CINDY *shakes her head. She turns and crosses to front door, taking out her keys.*

CINDY *(with finality)*
No! Good night, Chuck.

CHUCK *(off on another tangent)*
Your father doesn't like me. He thinks I've helled around too much, maybe . . .

CINDY

Please, Chuck!

CHUCK

Let's go in and talk it over with him. I . . .

CINDY *(in desperation)*
Please . . . please . . . *please!*

CHUCK *(with mingled disgust and defeat)*
OK, OK—all right, Cindy. I'm not coming in.

[CINDY *goes into the house, using door key.* HANK, *inside, back downstage a few steps toward Right end of sofa, holding the automatic in readiness.* CINDY *leans limply against the front door.* CHUCK *moves down the porch, then pauses, turns, looks at the house. His bafflement is clear on his face. Then he shakes his head and goes off down*

Right, swiftly. Through the following we hear the sound of his car motor starting, pulling away, receding. In the bedroom DAN *moves to the door, stands straining to hear what is happening in living room.* ROBISH *enters from the den, moves drunkenly to up Center; his voice, when he speaks, is heavier and louder than before, with only a suggestion of a blur in his words.* HANK *immediately conceals the gun.*

HANK *(glancing at Robish)*
Go on up, Miss.

[CINDY *crosses to steps, but* ROBISH *has planted himself in her path at the steps.* CINDY *glances from Robish to Hank.*

ROBISH

Have fun, sweetie? Parkin' with the boyfriend? Whatcha been doin'?

[CINDY *looks trapped;* DAN *opens the bedroom door a crack; as* ELEANOR *starts to ask a question he motions her to be quiet.*

HANK

Get back in there, Robish.

[DAN *steps out of bedroom.*

ROBISH

Who yah givin' orders now? *(To Cindy.)* Ain't been searched yet. Searched the old man, didn't we?

DAN *(barks)*
Griffin!

ROBISH

Lift your arms, baby. I'm gonna search you personal.

DAN *(comes down steps)*
Griffin!

[ROBISH *makes a drunken gesture to Dan behind him.*
HANK *takes a single step.*

HANK

Get out of her way, Robish!

[GLENN *appears in dining room door.*

DAN

Griffin, if you intend to let him get away with this . . .

GLENN *(revolver in hand now)*

Stay where you are, Hilliard!

ROBISH

Pretty little gal might try to sneak a gun in . . .

DAN

Griffin, you don't want to have to use that gun of yours,
do you?

GLENN *(grabs Robish)*

You goddam lunkhead . . .

ROBISH *(with one swing of his arm throws* GLENN *back
violently)*

Everybody givin' me orders! *(Steps toward Cindy.)* Lift
your arms, baby.

DAN

A shot'll be heard, Griffin . . .

[*But* HANK *moves fast now, steps in between Cindy and
Robish with the automatic drawn on Robish. There is a
pause.* ROBISH *stands blinking owlishly at the automatic.*

GLENN *(a breath)*

Hank . . . you damn fool.

ROBISH *(incredulously)*

Where'd ya get that?

HANK *(still covering Robish)*
You going up to bed now, miss?

ROBISH *(bawling)*
Where'd yuh get that gun?

GLENN *(shoves ROBISH toward dining room)*
Go sleep it off, Robish.

ROBISH *(turns at the dining-room door)*
Turnin' on me, huh? All of yuh. *(Drunkenly maudlin.)*
Turnin' on your ol' pal Robish. Okay. Ya wait. Ya-*all*
wait . . . *(He goes into the dining room.)*

GLENN
What's it to you, Hank

HANK *(muttering defensively; moving Right)*
It ain't safe to touch the women.

GLENN *(skeptically)*
Yeah? . . .

CINDY
Thank you . . . Hank . . .

HANK *(after the briefest sort of pause)*
Get the hell to bed.

GLENN *(taking a step toward Cindy)*
Don't get the idea you ain't gonna be searched, redhead.

[*At this moment there is a sound off Left: a door slamming. A slight pause as the significance of this sound
reaches* GLENN *in living room.*

GLENN *(swiftly)*
Christ! Cover 'em, Hank. *(Moves to dining-room door.)*
I gotta stop that fool! Let 'em have it if you have to.

[ELEANOR, *through the above action, has been watching
and listening from the open bedroom door. In the living*

room now both DAN *and* CINDY *turn toward* HANK, *who is at Right, with gun on them.*

HANK
Don't get the idea I wont . . .

ELEANOR
Dan?

DAN
Stay in there, Ellie . . . hear?

HANK *(a warning)*
Don't get any ideas now . . .

DAN *(to Cindy)*
Cindy! You look . . . *(He glances at Hank, then back to Cindy.)* Are you sick?

CINDY *(turns to Dan)*
No, I . . .

[*Her eyes meet* DAN'S. *Pause. And then* CINDY, *clutching her stomach, takes a few steps to Right end of sofa and collapses.* DAN *takes a step toward her. Holding to back of sofa, she sinks into it.* ELEANOR *comes down the steps.*

ELEANOR
Cindy!

HANK *(tensely)*
Don't move . . . either one of you.

DAN
Dammit, this child's sick. If there's any decency in you at all . . .

[HANK, *very uncertainly, moves toward Cindy, eyes on her. In the bedroom* RALPHIE *has moved to the door.* If you're trying to pull . . . *(*RALPHIE *slips into the hall, as* HANK *calls uncertainly.)* Glenn! *(*HANK *moves cau-*

tiously toward Cindy—as RALPHIE, *above, slips down the hall and into Cindy's bedroom at extreme Right, and disappears, closing the door.)* She's just scared, I guess . . . *(When Cindy's bedroom door closes.)* Glenn? *(But the hall is empty now;* HANK *bends over Cindy.)* No need to be scared, Miss. No need to . . .

[CINDY *moves with animal swiftness. She grasps* HANK'S *arm and sinks her teeth into his wrist, hard.* HANK *drops the automatic on the floor in front of Cindy. He utters a cry of pain and surprise and straightens up, holding his wrist.* DAN *moves in with his right arm encircling* HANK'S *shoulders, pinning his hands to his chest.* CINDY *picks up the automatic and stands ready to Left of down Center, facing upstage.* DAN *drags* HANK *to the front door and opens it.* HANK *calls for "Glenn," but* DAN *succeeds in pushing him out the door.* DAN *closes and locks the door as* CINDY *runs across the room to the light switch. She turns off the living-room lights.* NOTE: *This light cue is at the discretion of the director.* ELEANOR *stands, bewildered.*

DAN

Ellie! Get on the phone. (CINDY *crosses to hand Dan the gun.)* Cindy, lock the back door!

[CINDY *moves, fast, and disappears into the dining room.* ELEANOR *has turned to go up the steps; she happens to glance into master bedroom.*

ELEANOR

Ralphie . . . ?

DAN

Ellie, for God's sake get on the phone!

[*Even as he speaks, however, he is moving toward the phone in living room, Left of Left chair. Impatiently he dials the operator—as, in hall,* ELEANOR *opens door of Ralphie's bedroom and calls.*

ELEANOR *(not yet in panic)*
  Ralphie?

DAN *(dialling)*
  Stay away from the windows, everyone!

  [*But* ELEANOR *has dashed swiftly down the hall, panic clear now, as she looks into Cindy's bedroom.*

ELEANOR
  Ralphie!

DAN
  Operator! *Operator!*

  [CINDY *returns from dining room, as* ELEANOR, *in hall, stops, crying out.*

ELEANOR
  Dan, don't! For God's sake, don't, Dan! Ralphie's not in the house.

  [*Pause.* CINDY *and* DAN *freeze.* DAN *stands with the phone in his hands.*

OPERATOR *(in phone)*
  Operator. Operator. This is your operator. Your call, please? . . .

  [DAN *replaces the phone.*

DAN *(a whisper)*
  God Almighty.

CINDY
  Maybe he got away.

  [*Another pause, shorter; then* GLENN *appears outside, down Right with* RALPHIE. GLENN *has* RALPHIE'S *arm pinned behind him and holds the boy as a shield. They move to the porch.*

GLENN

    Hilliard! Can you hear me in there, Hilliard?

RALPHIE *(plaintively)*

    Dad! Dad, he's hurting my arm.

ELEANOR *(in terror)*

    Dan, was that Ralphie? *Was that Ralphie?*

DAN

    Stay up there, Ellie! *(Calling slightly louder and moving Right.)* Don't shout out there, Griffin! *(Then, lower.)* Cindy, take your mother to her room. If you hear a shot . . . make the call!

[DAN *goes to front door.* CINDY *goes up the steps.* ELEANOR *goes into the master bedroom and stands near the door.* CINDY *picks up the extension phone in the hall, but keeps her hand on the circuit breaker. She is tense, waiting, her attention turned toward the front door.*

GLENN *(a loud whisper)*

    We go now, Hilliard . . . they find the brat in a ditch. *(DAN unlocks and opens the door.)* Turn on the light. And toss out the automatic.

DAN

    Let the boy come in, Griffin.

GLENN

    Lights first. Then the gun. *(DAN turns on the living room light. Optional. Then he tosses the automatic out.* GLENN *pushes* RALPHIE *up the porch before him.)* You're both covered, Pop.

RALPHIE *(still defiant—enters living room)*

    I . . . I tried.

DAN *(gently)*

    So did I. Go to your mother now, son.

[RALPHIE *slips behind Dan and goes up steps and into the bedroom—where* ELEANOR *takes him into her arms on bed.* GLENN *speaks to* HANK, *who appears down Right.*

GLENN

Hank . . . pick up the automatic. And get the lunkhead inside.

[HANK *disappears down Right.* GLENN *moves into living room, stepping close to Dan and urging him down to sofa with short jabs of the gun.*

DAN

Cindy . . . go into the bedroom and close the door.

HANK *(off stage)*

On your feet, Robish.

[CINDY *crosses and enters bedroom, closes door, leans against it.*

GLENN *(follows Dan, who stops at Right end of sofa)*

Couldn't wait, could you, Pop?

[*As* HANK *appears on porch, urging a groggy* ROBISH *ahead of him;* ROBISH'S *head is aching from Glenn's blow.*

ROBISH *(as he enters through front door)*

What happened? Wha . . .

HANK

Shut up!

GLENN *(to Dan, filled with deep rage, but softly)*

Less'n a hour an' you couldn't wait! (ROBISH *flops onto upstage love seat and* HANK *moves to up Left of sofa, watching Glenn.*) I had to put Robish on ice for a while, Pop . . . cause he couldn't learn who was runnin' things aroun' here. I guess I gotta learn you, too.

[GLENN *strikes* DAN'S *left shoulder with his left fist,*

violently. Then he strikes a stomach blow with the pistol in his right hand. As DAN *doubles up,* GLENN *lifts the gun and brings it down across his head, forcing* DAN *downstage of Glenn and toward the Right chair.* DAN *falls to floor by Right chair. Then* GLENN *lifts the gun twice again, three violent blows across the head. All this is very silent. Those in the bedroom do not hear.* HANK *watches, fascinated and repulsed.* GLENN *straightens, looks across at Hank.* HANK *backs up and sits slowly on Left chair.* GLENN *locks the front door, places pistol in his belt and turns to look down at* DAN, *who is completely unconscious. The lights dim.*

VERY SLOW CURTAIN

THE DESPERATE HOURS

ACT TWO

ACT TWO

SHERIFF'S OFFICE

Outside the window, night. The clock reads 12:04.

CARSON, *seated at desk, plays solitaire.* WINSTON *sits curled up awkwardly on chair.* BARD *leans against files, thumbing through telephone-reports. A long pause.* CARSON *glances at his watch.*

CARSON
> It's another day . . . in case anyone's interested.

BARD
> There's a full moon, too. So what? *(Holding up the reports, moves to Center.)* Collect calls . . . person-to-person . . . pay stations. Would you believe this many people sit up talking on the telephone at night? Why the hell don't they go to bed? *(drops the reports on the desk.)*

WINSTON
> Why don't *we?*

CARSON *(picking up the reports)*
> You've got all the reasons right here . . . Sickness . . . impulse . . . birth . . . death . . . drunkenness . . . love . . . hate . . .

BARD
> What the hell're you . . . a poet or something?

CARSON
> It'll break, Bard. You can stretch a wire just so tight.

DUTCH'S VOICE *(on intercom)*
  Jess . . . that 11:02 person-to-person from Columbus to
  Blackstone 2726 . . .

BARD *(flipping intercom button)*
  Yeah, yeah?

DUTCH'S VOICE
  It was the daughter calling to say the honeymoon was
  already a huge success.

BARD
  Great!

DUTCH'S VOICE
  My theory is this Helen Laski found another guy and
  climbed in the hay.

  [BARD *flips off the intercom.* WINSTON *rises sleepily.*

WINSTON
  I'll be in the file room, flat on my face. *My* theory is this
  Helen Laski don't believe in telephones. Uses carrier
  pigeons. Has a secret compartment in her brassiere.

  [WINSTON *exits. Outside, a police siren is heard fading in
  and coming to a stop.*

CARSON *(shuffling cards)*
  You'd find double solitaire kind of restful.

BARD
  Carson, you deal me just one of those cards and I'm
  gonna report you to J. Edgar Hoover. *(Shaking his head
  but smiling faintly as he crosses Left.)* Isn't it just my
  luck to meet up with a character like you on a night like
  this?

CARSON *(turns in swivel-chair)*
  You're not such hot company yourself . . . Ten bucks

says they're in Denver . . . or New Orleans . . . or
Nome, Alaska, by now.

BARD

They're here.

CARSON

Who told you . . . that monkey on your back?

BARD *(striding downstage)*

I say they're here, Carson, because Glenn Griffin's got all
kinds of dark pockets in his mind . . . all kinds of weird
twists. *(Pacing.)* He's always acting, for one thing . . .
trying to live up to some phony picture he carries around
in that snarled-up brain of his . . . some stupid, child-
ish image of what a really clever criminal should be.

CARSON *(shrugs)*

Well, that's a good reason. It doesn't explain why he's in
town, but it's a good reason. Any others?

BARD *(faces Carson squarely)*

Carson, did you ever look into the eyes of one of those
crazy kids . . . and hear him say, "You got yours coming, copper"? Between his teeth . . . with his broken
jaw wired up tight . . . "I'll get you." *That's* why I
know he's here and that's why *I'm* going to get to him
before he gets to *me. (Turns away.)* Any objections,
Carson? *(Moves Left.)*

CARSON

No objections, Bard. But if we catch up with him . . .
our job's to arrest, if possible.

BARD *(whirls)*

You remindin' me who's actually in charge here, Carson?

CARSON

Something like that. My friends call me Harry. *(He goes
back to his cards.)*

BARD *(steps to Carson)*

    Well, I'll tell you right now . . . I'm making no promises
. . . Harry.

(DIMOUT)

HILLIARD HOME

Dimness, except in bedroom. GLENN *sits at front window
in living room. In the bedroom* DAN *lies across bed with his
head on Right end of bed.* ELEANOR *sits on edge of end of
bed.* DAN *has a damp towel placed over his forehead.* ELEANOR
*has a dry towel in her hand. During the following they speak
in whispers loud enough to be heard.*

ELEANOR

    Darling . . . can you hear me? I want you to promise.

DAN

    What? *(Dazedly.)* Oh. I must've dozed off. Isn't that
remarkable?

ELEANOR

    You needed it. I slipped off myself, just sitting here. But
I heard every sound . . . every car that went by.

    [DAN *stirs.*

DAN

    What time is it?

    [ELEANOR *glances at watch.*

ELEANOR

    After one . . .

DAN *(trying to sit up)*

    Midnight. He said mid . . .

ELEANOR

Shhh. Don't move. Listen. What you did—what you tried
—that was a foolish and terrible and wonderful thing . . .
(Shakes her head as though trying to clear it.) No, no,
that's not what I meant to say. Dan, you must never do
anything like that again. Ever. You . . . you might have
been killed. I want you to promise me now. Dan, are you
listening?

DAN

What're they doing down there? Why haven't they gone

ELEANOR

Dan, please. Nobody knows anything about what's happening here. Nobody in the world. We're all alone in this.
Dan, I'm pleading with you . . .

DAN

Ellie . . . how long has it been since I said I love you?

ELEANOR

Dan . . .

DAN

Why shouldn't a man say it? Why didn't I say it all the
time . . . over and over?

ELEANOR

You didn't need . . .

DAN

Ellie, why'm I so grouchy in the mornings? No, that's
not what I mean . . . I mean . . . what's the matter,
people don't laugh more? Waking up . . . seeing the
sun . . . That . . . that was a funny joke Ralphie told
. . . about the moron and the icebox.

ELEANOR *(smiling wanly)*

Not very . . .

DAN

All right, it was lousy. Is that any reason not to laugh? *(In awe.)* God . . . this morning. How many hours ago? It's . . . it's like looking back on something that happened . . . a whole lifetime ago. *(Reaches out his right hand to her face.)* Your face . . . darling, you're beautiful. Do you know that? I must've been deaf, dumb and blind. For years.

ELEANOR *(takes his hand in hers)*

Dan . . . you haven't promised.

[DAN *sits up with difficulty.*

DAN

Ellie . I can't. I'm feeling along a blank wall. In the dark. If I find a hole . . . or even a crack . . . I've got to explore it. There's light behind that wall, Ellie. I never knew how much. There was light there once and there's got to be light again!

ELEANOR

Dan, look at yourself. Your head. Next time . . . you don't know. *You don't know.* He'll kill you.

DAN *(grimly)*

He won't kill me as long as he needs me. *(Suddenly.)* You look so *tired.* Damn them! *(Gently.)* When this is over, we're going to have a maid here. A full-time maid.

ELEANOR

You wouldn't really like it, Dan. None of us like having strangers in the . . .

[*She breaks off, realizing what she is saying. Their eyes meet. Pause. Then, there is the sound of a branch cracking off a tree and brushing down the side of the house. She starts and crumples.* DAN *holds her. Below,* GLENN *looks out the living-room window.*

DAN

It's all right, dear. It's all right. Only one of those dead branches off the oak. *(He takes her into his arms.)* My God, Ellie . . . it's a jungle. We jump at nothing. That's how you slept, isn't it . . . like an animal in the . . .

[*The telephone rings.* GLENN *rises, turns on light.* DAN *and* ELEANOR *straighten and* DAN *goes to bedroom door without opening it.* HANK *enters from dining room, fast, and* GLENN *gestures him to the extension phone in hall as the phone rings again.* CINDY *opens door of Ralphie's bedroom and stands in doorway, as* HANK *reaches hall phone.*

HANK *(ready at the phone upstairs)*
All set, Glenn.

[HANK *takes up the phone after* GLENN *answers and stands staring at* CINDY *in the door of Ralphie's room as he listens.*

GLENN *(picks up the phone downstairs)*
Hello? . . . Put her on . . . Yeah, this is Mr. James. *Put her on!* . . . Hi, doll, what's up? . . . Where are you? . . . Mmm—okay, get this. That stuff you're carrying . . . put it in a envelope . . . an' take down this address . . . Daniel C. Hilliard . . .

[GLENN *continues, but his voice is under the following dialogue so that the address is not heard.*

HANK *(to Cindy, harshly)*
Stay inside an' shut the door, redhead.

[CINDY, *in defiance, doesn't move.*

ELEANOR
Dan, what is it?

DAN *(opening bedroom door)*
Shhh . . .

GLENN *(under above dialogue so that address is not heard)*
. . . 243 North Central Avenue . . . Soon's I get it,
we'll make tracks, doll . . . See you Louisville. You
know where.

[GLENN *hangs up.* HANK *replaces the extension phone
and comes down the steps and is about to go into the
dining room. He stops in door when* DAN *comes down the
steps.*

ELEANOR *(follows* DAN *to the bedroom door)*
Dan!

DAN *(as he comes down the steps)*
Griffin! Who was that? What's happening?

GLENN *(casually)*
Tell you in the morning, Pop . . . after breakfast.

DAN *(shocked)*
After break— You'll tell me now!

GLENN *(angry)*
What's another day, Pop? Get some shuteye. You're
gonna need it.

[GLENN *turns his back on Dan and walks toward the
window at Right.* DAN *starts toward Glenn.*

HANK
Glenn! Watch it!

[GLENN *whirls.* DAN *stops, looks at Hank, then at Glenn,
and turns and goes up the steps.* ELEANOR *moves into bedroom and stands waiting for Dan.* CINDY *goes into Ralphie's room and closes the door.* GLENN *goes to the window,*

picks up the road map from the chair, and stands in the window, studying it. HANK *moves toward Center.*

HANK

Glenn . . . we gotta get outa here.

GLENN *(studying map intently)*

Shut up a minute, willya?

[HANK *stands tensely at Right end of sofa.* DAN *has entered bedroom and he stands leaning against door, stunned, trying to comprehend the meaning of the phone call.*

DAN *(flatly . . . low)*

They're not going.

ELEANOR

Oh Dan, no!

DAN *(suddenly the violence in him mounts to a determined grimness)*

They're going!

[DAN *turns to the door.* ELEANOR *stops him. The following builds in intensity until they are almost snarling at each other.*

ELEANOR

Dan, you promised, you promised!

DAN *(erupting slightly)*

Ellie, don't tie my hands! I'm tied up enough already!

ELEANOR *(desperately)*

If you go down there now, something terrible is going to happen. I know it. I *feel* it.

DAN

How long can we go on sitting on top of a volcano?

ELEANOR *(takes his hand, tugging at him)*
Dan, you're going to lie down now! I'm telling you!

DAN *(shouting, throws her off)*
You're not telling me what to do! *(Pause. They are appalled. They stand looking at each other for a moment. Then they go into each other's arms.* DAN *says, almost whispering.)* Ellie, what're we doing? What're we *doing?* *(Slight pause.)* How can he know, that scum down there . . . how can he know how to do this? A boy who never loved anyone in his life.

[ELEANOR *turns and sits on bed.* DAN *sinks down beside her, his arm around her, and they sit very quietly, not moving, through the following. In the living room* HANK *takes another steps toward Glenn.*

HANK
Glenn . . . what if they trace that call?

[GLENN *folds map and shoves it into a hip pocket; he is grinning, satisfied.*

GLENN
You ever hear of a burg called Circleville, Ohio? It's nineteen miles south-a Columbus. Them dumb coppers might be tracin' calls outta Columbus, Hank, but not outta no jerktown like Circleville.

HANK *(sits on Right arm of sofa)*
We'd be better off anywhere but here.

GLENN
It can't be nowhere else but here. With that much dough . . . in this town . . . I can have that copper put on ice for good.

HANK *(shaking his head)*
That one idea . . .

GLENN

Yeah, that one idea. Kid, you gotta stick with me on this.
You're . . . Hank, you're all I got. You know that. It's
you'n me against 'em all!

HANK *(trapped: conflicting emotions. He turns away.)*
I know, I know . . .

[GLENN *grabs him, turns him around.*

GLENN

You know . . . you know! You don't know nothin'! I
gotta get this outta my brain. I gotta sleep again. You
didn't lay in that bed . . . pain twistin' down in your
gut . . . months . . . jaw clamped up in a vise . . .
eatin' that slop through a tube . . . months . . . till
pretty soon there ain't nothin' in your mind but the face-a
the guy that done it. Me with my hands up . . . tossin'
out my gun . . . and that bastard walkin' up'n cloutin'
me. I can still hear the way the bone cracked . . . *An'
me with my hands up!*

(BLACKOUT)

SHERIFF'S OFFICE

Clock: 6:15. Early morning. CARSON *is seated Left.* BARD
*is rising from swivel chair and he moves downstage through
the following.*

BARD

Yeah, he had his hands up. Trying to surrender. *After* he'd
plugged one of the best damn cops ever walked. While
Jerry was laying there twisting and screaming in the
gutter . . . with a bullet in a nerve . . . *then* Griffin
throws out his empty gun and steps out of the doorway of

that hotel, big as life. Only I didn't let him get away
with it. I let him have it. One crack . . . right in that
grinning face of his. *(Rubbing his fist.)* If I'd only
arrested him . . . or shot him before he gave up . . .
he'd probably've forgotten it. But according to *his* warped
code, I double-crossed *him*.

CARSON *(quietly)*
Under the circumstances . . . police code, too.

BARD
Listen! That kid's as ruthless as they come! He'd as soon
kill a human being as step on a bug.

CARSON
All right . . . so civilization didn't take. In his case. But
we've climbed a long way out of the slime, Jess. Maybe
that slime still clings to some of us. *Them.* But you're a
police officer, Jess . . . and civilized men can't let the
slime on *them* drag *us* back down. If we don't live by
the rules, the rules will soon disappear. Then . . .
(Shrugs.) we're all right back where we started.

BARD
Rules! He was sentenced to ten years. He'd have been
out again anyway inside of three more.

CARSON
Which only proves it's a pretty ramshackle system. But
it's all we've got. You had no right to break his jaw. And
if we find him, you've no right to kill him unless it's the
only way to stop him.

BARD *(sits on edge of desk; bitterly)*
Sure, send him back to that cardboard prison . . . so
he can start all over again.

CARSON
No choice, Jess. Unless you want to become just like him.

In that case, he wins, anyway. *(Rises.)* I'm ready for breakfast. How about you?

[BARD, *thoughtful for a moment, looks at Carson, rises.*

BARD
   Yeah.

(DIMOUT)

HILLIARD HOME

It is morning. ELEANOR *is seated on the sofa,* RALPHIE *beside her.* HANK *stands at the window, smoking.* DAN *is entering from the dining room, followed by* GLENN. GLENN *picks his teeth with finger and wipes hand on sofa as he crosses to Right.*

GLENN
   Lady, that 'as a goddam good breakfast. *(Takes Hank's cigarette, turns to Dan.)* Hilliard, you ever broke, your woman can support you good. Cookin'. *(Takes a drag on the cigarette and returns it to Hank.)*

DAN *(up Left of sofa)*
   How much longer, Griffin?

GLENN
   Hell, you don't have any worse headache'n Robish 'n there . . . *(Gestures into the den.)* and he's nursin' a hangover to boot.

DAN *(level and insistent—as he moves to down Left of sofa)*
   How long?

GLENN
   Till I get a certain envelope in the mail. Meantime . . .

everything goes on just like before aroun' here. You'n the redhead go to work.

HANK

Glenn, if he's gonna be gone all day outta the house . . .

GLENN

You don't trust Hilliard, Hank? *(Crosses to face Dan.)* Now me—I trust the old gink. You know why? I got him where the hair's short, that's why. Junior here gets a break. He misses a day of school. (CINDY *comes out of her room and down the hall.)* Won't hurt you none, kid. Missed a few myself.

CINDY *(on steps; scornfully)*

And look at you.

RALPHIE

I'd just as soon go . . .

GLENN *(crosses to Cindy around Right end of sofa)*

Yeah, you're lookin', Sis. Pass you on the street, you'd look right through us both. You're seein' us now, red-head.

CINDY

No comment.

GLENN *(to Dan—as he crosses angrily to up of sofa)*

Now, get the lead outta your . . .

[*The thud of the newspaper is heard against the front door. The* HILLIARDS *are not startled but* GLENN *and* HANK *jump into action.* HANK, *drawing the automatic, moves up to the door.* GLENN, *with the .38 ready, covers the family and backs to down Left.* HANK *unlocks and opens the door a crack. He kneels down and reaches out with his left hand to bring in the paper.* HANK *rises, closing the door, and tosses the paper to Glenn.* GLENN *unfolds the paper.* HANK *locks the door.* RALPHIE, *who has been watching it all, snickers.*

GLENN *(after a split-second pause)*
Get your kicks young, kid. *(To Dan.)* You don't want to be late for that time-clock, Pop.

[ELEANOR *rises and crosess to Glenn, fire in her eyes.*

ELEANOR
Why do you want to go on torturing my husband? You know what he'll be thinking . . . wondering . . . imagining . . . in that office! You take pleasure in torturing him, don't you?

GLENN *(easily)*
Lady, I take pleasure in looking out for my own skin . . . and Hank's.

DAN *(in warning)*
Ellie . . .

ELEANOR
No, no, it's some sort of cruel, inhuman, sadistic game with you. You're playing a *game!*

[*Abruptly, she explodes into violence; slaps Glenn full across the face.* DAN *steps in, grabs her and swings her around, then turns to look at Glenn. The family is in a small group, defiant. Long pause, while* GLENN *rubs his jaw.*

GLENN *(quietly)*
Whose family gettin' tough this morning. Nothin' personal, ma'am.

DAN *(grimly—knowing)*
It's personal all right. In some strange mixed-up way.

GLENN
Clickety-click. Don't get ulcers tryin' to dope it, Pop. *(To*

Cindy.) You, redhead. Keep that pretty mouth shut to-day, see. Or that boy friend of yours ain't gonna want to take you on no more rides. Not after Robish gets done with you.

[*Pause.*

DAN *(deciding—a step to Glenn)*
I'm not leaving this house today.

GLENN *(hardening)*
You ain't learned yet who's runnin' it?

HANK
Glenn, I think . . .

GLENN *(exploding)*
You think! With what? I'm lookin' out for you, you slobberin' pukin' little bastard. (GLENN *turns to Dan.)* You ain't had nothin', Pop. Nothin' like what you deserve.

DAN
Deserve? . . .

GLENN
Yeah . . . deserve! You'n your fancy carpet and your big lawn'n your goddam snazzy car!

DAN *(takes a step toward Glenn)*
Griffin . . . (ELEANOR *touches Dan's arm to restrain him but he pulls away and continues.)* you're not going to take it out on me and my family because you hate the world! I've worked for every cent I ever made . . . worked hard . . . for this house, that car . . . and I'm proud of it. That table you've scarred with your whisky . . . the furniture you've wiped your filthy hands on . . . the carpet you've burnt holes in. Proud because I *did* work **for it!**

GLENN *(spits on carpet with contempt)*
Sucker! Just like our old man, ain't he, Hank?

DAN
I pity the poor man!

GLENN
Don't waste your time. He kicked off while we was in reform school. He was a *proud* bastard, too. Now get outta here!

DAN
I'm staying right here!

GLENN *(violent)*
Hilliard, I told you . . . *(Changes—shrugs.)* Okay . . . *(Sits on Left chair.)* Okay . . . You stay . . . an' we stay. 'Cause we ain't gonna beat it outta here till we get that dough. An' that dough's in a letter . . . addressed to you . . . at your office. *(Pause. The fight goes out of Dan.)* We don't want no Federal men tracin' anything up to your front door here, do we? . . . See, Pop, I'm thinkin' of you.

[ELEANOR *takes Dan's arm.*

ELEANOR
He'll go. He's going. *(As CINDY moves to love seat and gets her own coat and brings Dan's coat to him.)* Dan, I'll be upstairs with Ralphie. If one of them starts up the stairs, I'll scream so loud they'll *have* to use their guns. That'll be the end of it. For them too. Now I'll get your coat. It's getting colder every minute . . .

[CINDY *already stands waiting with Dan's coat.*

DAN
I . . . I can hold my own coat, Cindy.

CINDY

Maybe I'd *like* to hold your coat.

[DAN *climbs into coat, then turns to Eleanor.*

ELEANOR

Careful now, Dan . . . I know, I say that every morning of the world, don't I?

[DAN *takes* ELEANOR *in his arms. They kiss . . . with great meaning and tenderness, in sharp contrast to yesterday morning's casual good-bye.* GLENN *makes a kissing sound with his mouth, then makes a pop with his finger in his mouth.* HANK *takes a step down as* GLENN *laughs mockingly.*

HANK

What's so funny? (*As* GLENN *frowns, the laughter dying.*) I don't see nothin' so funny, you should break your neck laughin'.

GLENN

I laugh when I feel like it. You don't have a goddam thing to say about it. That right? . . . That right, Hank?

HANK (*dropping into chair*)

I never had nothin' to say about anything.

[DAN *moves toward front door.* CINDY *steps to Ralphie, tousles his hair.*

CINDY (*softly, fondly*)

Mister Pest to you.

GLENN

You, Hilliard. (*Rises and crosses to up of sofa.*) That nick on your head—you got a story ready? 'Cause it wouldn't take much of a slip today, Pop. Just a little one and . . . you're gonna wish you never come back through that door.

DAN *(quietly . . . with dignity and force as he turns to see Glenn)*
Griffin . . . you're staying here now for only one reason. To get a man killed. A man who did something to you. I couldn't understand that before. Now I can. I understand it because I'm more like you now than you know. If any harm comes to anyone in this house, Griffin, I'm going to kill you. Me. No matter what it takes . . . whether the police capture you first or not . . . if it takes my whole life, Griffin, I'll find you and I'll kill you. Do you understand that?

GLENN *(impressed but attempting swagger)*
Pop . . . you're a regular comedian.

DAN
Do you understand that?

GLENN
Sure, Pop . . . I got you all the way. *(Turns away, steps toward Left.)*

DAN
And if not you, Griffin . . . your brother.

GLENN *(immediately tense, violent—whirls)*
You come near Hank and . . .

DAN *(firmly)*
That's the deal, Griffin. That's the deal. You've turned me into your kind of animal now.

[GLENN *does not move.* DAN *turns, takes a long look at Ralphie, then Eleanor.* CINDY *opens the door.* DAN *follows* CINDY *out, closing the door behind him; they exit from porch to Right.*

GLENN *(moving down Left)*
Lady . . . you didn't know what a tough old bird you married, did you?

ELEANOR *(softly)*
No. No, I didn't.

[ELEANOR *nods to* RALPHIE, *who rises and joins her;
through the following dialogue they go up the steps and
into the bedroom.*

HANK
Glenn . . . why're you crowdin' it? Why go on takin'
these chances?

GLENN
You don't take chances, you might's well be dead.

HANK *(rising)*
That's what we gonna be . . . all of us . . . this keeps
up.

[*During the preceding dialogue SOUND of old truck
approaching.*

GLENN
You start yammerin' again, I'm gonna give you a belt
across . . .

[*They hear the truck. Immediate tension. In bedroom*
ELEANOR *crosses to window, looks out.* GLENN *rushes to
the window at Right, looks out.* HANK *rushes across the
stage and exits into dining room.*
Hey lady . . . lady, who is that?

[ELEANOR *comes to bedroom door, stands in hall.* RALPHIE
looks out window.

ELEANOR
It's . . . only Mr. Patterson. He hauls away the trash

[GLENN *thinks this over a second.*

GLENN
Okay . . . Okay, let him get it and clear out.

ELEANOR *(now on steps)*
Only . . . he'll . . . it's the end of the month. He'll come to the door to collect.

GLENN
Damn! *(Steps to door of den.)* Robish! *(Then crosses to dining-room door.)* Hank!

[ROBISH *enters from den; he is suffering from a hangover and from last night's violence. He sits in Right chair, still groggy.*

ROBISH
Wha's goin' on?

[HANK *enters from dining room, fast.*

HANK
He's puttin' the trash in his truck, Glenn.

GLENN *(to Eleanor)*
Okay, lady, you pay him. Go tell him to come round to the front door.

[ELEANOR *exits into dining room.*

GLENN *(to Hank)*
Stick with her. *(Steps up the steps, calls to Ralphie.)* Hey kid—out here where I can see you.

(RALPHIE *reluctantly moves into hall from bedroom as* GLENN *turns down the steps.*

ELEANOR'S VOICE
Oh yes, Mr. Patterson. Come around to the other door, will you?

ROBISH
My gut's growlin'.

GLENN *(tensely, gun out)*
Knock off.

[ELEANOR *enters from dining room with checkbook and pen. She sits on Left chair and scribbles a check, nervously.* GLENN *steps to her.*

GLENN

You always pay the old gink with a check?

ROBISH *(voice blurred)*

Who is it?

ELEANOR *(writing)*

Yes. Yes. My husband . . . *(Then firmly.)* my husband thinks it's not safe to have too much cash in the house. *(Signs.)* That's funny, isn't it?

[MR. PATTERSON—*old, wearing overalls—appears on the front porch, crosses to front door. He knocks.* ROBISH *leaps up and moves up of front door.*

GLENN *(a whisper)*

Snap it up. *(To Hank.)* Stick with the brat.

[HANK *goes up steps and into bedroom with* RALPHIE.

ELEANOR

I'm coming, Mr. Patterson. *(Rises.)* Ralphie . . . not a word out of you now.

[*Crosses to front door, but* GLENN *stops her, takes check, turns it over, examines it swiftly, hands it back and moves up the steps, gun ready.* HANK *listens at bedroom door.*

ELEANOR *opens front door.*

MR. PATTERSON

Mornin', Mrs. Hilliard. Nasty day, turnin' into, ain't it? *(Takes check.)* Thank you kindly, Mrs. Hilliard. You . . . *(Stops.)* Say . . . you feelin' yourself, Mrs. Hilliard?

ELEANOR

Yes, I . . . only a slight cold. Nothing . . .

MR. PATTERSON
Yep, lotsa colds aroun'. Folks don't seem to know what to do for 'em these days. Call 'em virus. Now me, whenever I get—

ELEANOR
Goodbye, Mr. Patterson.

MR. PATTERSON
Your daughter buy herself another of them second-hand cars, Mrs. Hilliard?

[GLENN *tenses.* ELEANOR *half-turns away, at a loss.*

ELEANOR
Cindy? No, no!

[*Abruptly, in panic, she closes door in* MR. PATTERSON'S *face. He stands looking at it, placing check in his billfold.* ROBISH *crosses swiftly into dining room, muttering, and* GLENN *springs to window Right. In bedroom,* HANK *looks out window.*

ROBISH
What's 'at joker doin' here?

ELEANOR
He only thinks Cindy has another car. He . . .

HANK'S VOICE
Hey, Glenn!

[GLENN *starts swiftly to Left.*

ELEANOR
Mr. Patterson wouldn't suspect anything. He . . .

GLENN *(crossing)*
Shut up!

HANK
He's snoopin' around the garage, Glenn.

[GLENN *exits into dining room.* HANK *moves out of bedroom and down the steps.*

ELEANOR *(faintly—as she moves to sofa weakly)*
Oh no. He's only taking the trash from the containers alongside.

HANK *(crossing to Right window and looking out)*
Up on his toes lookin' in the windows?

ELEANOR
On Thursday mornings he always . . .

[ROBISH *enters from dining room and lumbers over to the front window at Right.*

ROBISH
That joker wrote something down.

ELEANOR
Oh no, I'm sure . . .

[GLENN *enters and stands at dining room door, uncertain, frowning, momentarily bewildered as to what to do.* HANK *crosses to him.*

HANK
Robish said he wrote something down—?

GLENN *(slowly; uncertain, glancing at Eleanor)*
He wrote down the license number.

[*Outside, SOUND of truck motor whirring, starting.*

ROBISH
He's goin'. *(Crosses down of sofa to Center.)* Fork over the gun, Griffin.

ELEANOR
I'm sure he only . . .

GLENN
Shut up, both-a you, I'm thinkin'.

[*As truck motor becomes louder, sputtering.*

ROBISH
Gimme the gun I can hop on the back-a the truck.

HANK
Glenn! Listen! We . . .

ROBISH
You want that old gink goin' to the coppers?

[*As the truck motor fails and tries again,* GLENN, *with smile of defiance and revenge at Hank, hands Robish the gun, and* ROBISH *starts for front door.* GLENN *grabs him.*

GLENN
You call me on the phone. An' stay outta sight. I'll have Hilliard bring you back. Use your head for a change.

ROBISH (*wrenches himself free and crosses to front door. Truck motor starts again.*)
My head feels better already!

[ROBISH *goes out front door and across porch on the run, full of glee. The truck motor pulls away, recedes through following.* HANK *looks pale and sick.* ELEANOR, *stunned, sinks to sofa, beginning to weep.*

ELEANOR
He . . . he knew nothing. (*Corrects self.*) *Knows* nothing.

HANK (*steps to Glenn*)
Glenn, are you crazy? Hilliard won't bring Robish back in here.

GLENN
He will when I'm done with him on the phone. Pop don't

want Robish picked up any more'n we do . . . an' tippin'
the cops this address. *(Suddenly grabs Hank.)* What's the
matter with you anyway, kid? You got a weak stomach
after all? (HANK *turns his head away.)* What're you
stewin' about? You're free, ain't you?

HANK *(wrenches himself loose, starts for dining room)*
I was free-er in that cell!

[HANK *goes into the dining room; he slams the door.*
GLENN *is baffled and angry.*

GLENN *(to Eleanor)*
Lady! Shut up that wailin'! Go some place else'n cry!

[ELEANOR *rises slowly and, with difficulty, mounts the
steps.*

ELEANOR
Poor man . . . that poor old man . . . he wouldn't hurt
a fly.

(DIMOUT)

SHERIFF'S OFFICE

Darkness outside. WINSTON *is seated at desk.* BARD *is
pacing, steps down Left.*

BARD
Who'd want to pump three slugs in the back of an innocent old guy like that?

WINSTON
Who can say? Somebody settling an old score . . . old
crony he cheated at cards . . .

BARD *(turns)*
Sixty-three years old, half-crippled with arthritis . . .
wouldn't harm a fly. (BARD *looks up as* FREDERICKS *enters
and moves to Center.* LT. FREDERICKS *is an older man,
crisp and efficient, with a weathered face. He wears a
State Police uniform.* WINSTON *rises.)* Fredericks, are we
going to get that stuff from the state's attorney's office or
aren't we?

FREDERICKS
Carson's prying it out of them. Bard, why make so much
of an old garbage man gettin' bumped?

BARD
He was killed by a .38. The prison guard at Terre
Haute . . .

FREDERICKS
Sure, there's only one .38 in the state! Deputy, you got
a obsession. You can't tie in every crime in the area with
those three.

BARD
I reckon not, Lieutenant. Only *you* tell *me* why anybody'd . . . *(Breaks off as* CARSON *enters and crosses to
desk.)* Well, Carson?

[WINSTON *moves upstage of desk chair.*

CARSON *(tearing the top off large manila envelope which he
has brought in, emptying the contents on the desk during
the following)*
Claude Patterson died at the hands of person or persons
unknown. All I've got is the junk the old man was carrying in his pockets when they found the body. *(Handling
the items, handing checks to* BARD *who steps in.)* Checks
. . . Seventeen one-dollar bills . . . Ball-point pen . . .
A snuff box . . . Wallet . . . Usual stuff. Driver's li-

cense . . . Photograph of a young girl, taken forty years ago, at least.

BARD *(examining checks)*

Checks made out to Claude Patterson, some to cash. Thirteen for three dollars, two for six bucks.

WINSTON

The guy made more'n I do.

CARSON

Some scraps of paper . . .

[BARD *smoothes them out during the following as he moves to Left with checks and scraps of paper.*

WINSTON *(to Carson)*

How long ago do they figure it happened?

CARSON

Before noon, coroner said. Old man must've run into the woods from the truck. A hunter came across the body just before dusk. City police found the truck parked alongside a service station other side of . . .

BARD *(very, very quietly)*

Hold it. *(Low whistle of amazement between teeth as others turn.)* God. Look't this . . . *(As others cross to examine the scrap of paper.)* State's attorney's office examined this stuff?

CARSON *(as he looks at paper)*

That was my impression. *(Then softly, too.)* Good Lord!

WINSTON *(an excited whisper)*

Patterson might've got just a quick glance. In a hurry, y'know . . .

FREDERICKS *(cynically)*

He heard it on the radio . . . jotted it down just in case.

WINSTON

    But if you change that 3 to a 8, you got it. Maybe his eyes . . . a old man like that . . .

BARD *(thoughtfully)*

    Or there was mud on the plate.

WINSTON

    Jesse, if you change that 3 to a 8, you got it!

BARD *(with throb in voice)*

    Just for a while . . . just for a little while now . . . we're *going* to change that 3 to an 8. We'll just kinda pretend Mr. Patterson didn't *own* a radio. We're gonna pretend he saw that license, Tom . . . these checks. *(Hands them to Winston.)* Start working backwards! Names, addresses, telephone numbers, where they work. Everything!

[WINSTON *starts out.*

FREDERICKS

    Sure, let's go on a wild-goose chase . . . break the monotony.

[WINSTON *stops.*

BARD

    Those were the last people saw him alive. These and whatever other customers live in that neighborhood. Let's find that neighborhood and let's scour it down with a wire brush.

WINSTON

    Go ahead, Jess, say it.

BARD

    I don't like to say it, Tom . . .

WINSTON
      Say it, Jess. *(To Carson as he exits.)* He was right . . .
      This is it!

BARD *(crosses to desk)*
      God, it might be. Right here in town!

FREDERICKS
      You want any more troopers on it, lemme know. My men
      got nothing else to do. *(He exits.)*

BARD *(sitting at the desk)*
      Any bets now, Carson? Any bets that beat-up gray car
      isn't in that neighborhood somewhere? Any bets, Harry?

CARSON
      No bets, Jess.

BARD *(flips intercom, speaks into it)*
      Dutch. Get me a city map in here. And a city directory!
      (Flips off intercom. To Carson.) Now. If only we can get
      to 'em before some other innocent citizen stumbles across
      their path . . .

                    (BLACKOUT)

                  HILLIARD HOME

      Evening. The door chimes are sounding. ELEANOR *is Right
of Center, stands facing the door.* GLENN *is down of Right
window, looking out, and as the chimes sound again he moves
swiftly to den, gesturing to* ELEANOR *to open the door.* HANK,
at dining-room door, backs into dining room. MISS SWIFT,
youngish and pert, stands on front porch, ringing the bell.

      In the bedroom RALPHIE *stands at the door, straining to
listen.*

GLENN *(in whisper)*
Okay, lady . . . only be careful.

[GLENN *goes into den.* ELEANOR *takes a deep breath and opens the door.* MISS SWIFT *pushes into the room.*

MISS SWIFT
Good evening, Mrs. Hilliard. I've come to see Ralph.

ELEANOR *(standing with the door open wide)*
Oh . . . yes. *(Glances nervously toward dining room.)* Yes . . . *(Speaks for Glenn's benefit.)* Ralphie, it's your *teacher*, Miss Swift.

[ELEANOR *closes the door.*

MISS SWIFT *(as she moves down to sofa)*
You see, Ralph so rarely misses a day at school that I thought I'd drop by to . . . *(She stops, looking at the disordered room; her manner changes.)* I . . . I daresay I should have telephoned first.

ELEANOR *(nervously—as she crosses to Right end of sofa)*
Oh, no, no, that's perfectly all . . . *(Abruptly.)* Please sit down.

MISS SWIFT *(sits on sofa)*
I do hope that Ralph isn't seriously ill . . . *(She realizes that she is sitting on an uncomfortable object, reaches back and brings out the empty whisky bottle, which she places on the coffee table.)*

ELEANOR *(with a valiant effort at control)*
Only . . . just a cold. But we thought it best not to expose the other children.

[*Through the following,* RALPHIE *slips stealthily from bedroom into hall, then into his own bedroom, leaving door slightly ajar.*

MISS SWIFT
   My dear Mrs. Hilliard, there is no such thing as a cold.
   Have you had a doctor's opinion?

ELEANOR
   No. That is, we thought we could doctor it ourselves . . .

MISS SWIFT
   Mrs. Hilliard, how could you *possibly* doctor it yourself
   if you're convinced it's a *cold?* One member of a class
   stays home one day, and whoosh, it goes through the
   entire room. Not the germs, you understand, but the *idea*
   of the germs. *(She rises and moves quickly to steps.)* Perhaps I'd better have a look at him myself.

   [ELEANOR *moves fast and stops* MISS SWIFT *on the first
   step.*

ELEANOR
   No, you can't!

RALPHIE *(calling from his room)*
   I'll be down in a minute, Miss Swift!

MISS SWIFT *(bewildered)*
   Well, of course, if I've come at an inopportune . . .

RALPHIE
   I'm just finishing my composition!

   [CINDY *appears on porch, approaches front door, followed
   by* DAN *and* ROBISH.

MISS SWIFT
   Your son, Mrs. Hilliard, is going to be a brilliant author
   some day. *(Turning as* CINDY, DAN *and* ROBISH *enter.)*
   You mark my . . . *(Her voice trails off as she stares.*
   CINDY *stops and moves upstage.* ROBISH, *after a startled
   glance at Miss Swift, turns to door and stands with his
   back to the room.* DAN *steps up of sofa, puzzled, immedi-*

ately alert, glancing from dining-room door to door of den.)
Mr. Hilliard?

ELEANOR
Dan, you . . . uh . . . remember Miss Swift. Ralphie's
teacher! (Calling desperately.) Ralphie, are you *coming?*

DAN
Sure I remember. How're you, Miss Swift?

ELEANOR
Miss Swift . . . dropped in to see how Ralphie was feeling.

As MISS SWIFT *stares at* DAN, *he makes his decision. He
is drunk! He immediately goes into a muted drunk act,
turns to Robish.*

DAN
She did, did she? What do you think of that . . . Johnny? That's what I call a nice little old PTA practice.
(Ushering ROBISH *toward the dining room.)* You know
where I keep it, Johnny. Help yourself. (MISS SWIFT *stares
at* ROBISH *as he, keeping his face turned away from her,
moves into the dining room.* DAN *turns at dining-room
door.)* Met old pal Johnny at a . . . *(Turns to Cindy.)*
Cindy, say hello to Miss Swift. (CINDY *and* MISS SWIFT
exchange nods. DAN *sits on sofa.)* Whew, has Cindy been
laying it to me! Leave it to Cindy to know where to find
her old man.

[RALPHIE *opens door of his room, appears, composition
book in hand.*

DAN *(picks up whisky bottle from end table and upends it
into coffee cup)*
Where does the stuff go in this house? *(He lays the bottle
flat on the table.)*

RALPHIE *(on step above Miss Swift)*
I . . . I finished my composition for this week, Miss Swift.

MISS SWIFT *(nonplussed, takes composition book)*
I'll . . . I'll see that you get full credit, Ralph.

[*She turns and steps down one step, but* DAN *stops her, stepping in close.*

DAN *(in commanding tone)*
Miss Swift! I'll take that, please. *(He takes the composition book from her hands rudely, opens it and reads, then looks up at* RALPHIE, *who turns and runs into master bedroom, where he stands listening at the partly-closed door.)* So . . . so this is what they call a composition nowadays. You . . . you encourage such drivel, Miss Swift?

MISS SWIFT
Mr. Hilliard . . . in all fairness . . . I don't think you're in any condition to discuss *any*thing tonight.

DAN
In that case, I'll read it in the morning.

[MISS SWIFT *glances at bedroom door, then crosses to Eleanor, places a hand on her arm.*

MISS SWIFT
Mrs. Hilliard, let me assure you that what I've seen here tonight will in no way affect my belief in Ralph.

[*After a glance back at Dan, she goes quickly to the front door, opens it, and marches out, closing the door. She crosses porch and disappears. Immediately,* GLENN *rushes in from the den and to the front door and locks it, then moves to the window and stands looking out.* ELEANOR *crosses toward* DAN, *who sinks into the Left chair.* ROBISH *enters from the dining room, followed by* HANK.

ELEANOR
Oh, Dan . . . Dan, how did you ever? . . .

ROBISH
Griffin, we gotta stop that dame!

HANK
Sure, Robish . . . shoot up the whole town!

ROBISH
She seen me!

DAN
She wasn't looking at you!

GLENN *(moves to Right end of sofa)*
Old guy's right, Robish. Hilliard took her mind offa you. *(Crosses to down Center.)* Come 'ere, Pop. *(As* DAN *rises and crosses to face Glenn down Center.)* Gotta hand it to you, Hilliard. (GLENN *frisks him, carefully.)* You had that dame in a real stew. You'd of made a great con man. *(To Eleanor.)* Get up there with that smart brat.

[ELEANOR *goes up the steps and into bedroom . . . sinks to bed, next to Ralphie.* GLENN *moves past Dan to face Robish Left of Center.* HANK *crosses to window at Right, as* DAN *turns to watch Glenn.*

HANK
Glenn . . . this is goin' on too long.

GLENN *(ignoring Hank)*
Robish, did you get that piece of paper outta the old guy's pocket?

ROBISH
Couldn't. He jumped outta the truck.

GLENN
You dumb goddam . . .

ROBISH *(displaying the pistol)*
  He didn't get far.

GLENN *(reaching for it)*
  I'll take the .38 now, Robish.

ROBISH *(holds it away)*
  I kinda like th' feel of it.

  [*Pause . . . a silent duel.*

GLENN *(an effort to hold his command)*
  Get on the back door.

ROBISH

  Get on the back door yourself, Griffin. Stuff it!

  [ROBISH *laughs defiantly, pockets the gun and sits in Left chair.*

DAN

  Griffin . . . the money didn't come to the office today.

GLENN *(his mind on Robish and the gun)*
  Dope it yourself, Pop, you're so smart.

DAN

  You didn't really expect it.

GLENN

  Mail takes time. You should-a thought of that. It wasn't mailed till early this mornin'. *(Grinning, turns to Dan.)* Ought to get here some time tomorrow.

  [*Pause. General shock.*

HANK *(bleakly)*
  Tomorrow?

DAN *(to Glenn—angrily)*
  Why, you young . . .

GLENN

Take it easy, Pop . . . 'n stay healthy. *(To Hank.)*
Yeah . . . tomorrow. What's one more night?

HANK *(low)*

Christ!

DAN

Griffin, I've played your filthy game up to now . . . **but**
by bringing that ape back here after he killed a man . . .

ROBISH *(threatening, under his breath)*

Who you callin' a ape?

DAN

. . . . we're accessories now.

GLENN

That's right, Hilliard. You're on our side now. *(Crosses
to Hank at Right.)* I'll take the automatic, kid.

[*Slight pause.* HANK *faces Glenn.*

HANK

I'm hangin' onto it.

[*Longer pause. Slowly,* GLENN *turns from Hank to Dan.*
ROBISH *snorts a short laugh.*

GLENN

How you like that, Pop? They both got the guns. *(Half-
turns to Hank.)* Only they ain't got half a brain between
'em. Without me, they're cooked . . . an' they know it.
(GLENN *turns on Cindy, moving toward her upstage of
sofa)* You didn't feel like blabberin' to the boy friend,
did you, sweetie?

CINDY *(holding her ground)*

I felt like it. But I didn't. I'll explain it the night you
take your walk to the electric chair.

[GLENN's *tension has been growing. He explodes.* HANK

*turns from the window and steps toward Cindy up
Center.*

GLENN *(threateningly, to* CINDY, *who backs away)*
There're ways of shuttin' that pretty face of yours, redhead!

HANK
If you didn't tell him, what's the boy friend doin' drivin'
past the house out there . . . slow?

GLENN *(taut, tense—as he springs to front door, opens it a
crack)*
If you pulled a fast one, spitfire . . .

HANK *(in panic)*
Glenn, listen!

[ROBISH *rises.*

GLENN
Lemme think, willya?

HANK
Glenn! They're not gonna stop comin' to the door!

GLENN *(turning to him)*
Yellow, Hank?

HANK
Yeah . . . okay . . . yellow! *They're not gonna stop
coming to the door!*

(BLACKOUT)

SHERIFF'S OFFICE

*Clock: 8:25. There is a map of Indianapolis on the wall
and an area has been marked off with heavy crayon.*

FREDERICKS *is studying the map.* BARD *is speaking over the radio.*

BARD

We're looking at a map of the neighborhood, Tom. Where are you?

WINSTON'S VOICE

Parked behind a service station. Corner of Kessler Boulevard and Keystone. *(As* FREDERICKS *marks an X on the map location.)* The main roads are covered. The other cars're just where you put 'em. It's a high-toned sort of neighborhood, Jess.

BARD

Okay. Now. Let's start knocking on a few high-toned doors!

FREDERICKS *(steps down)*

Bard . . . they're over two hundred houses in that area. It'll take all night and part of tomorrow . . .

BARD *(ignoring Fredericks)*

Every one of the trashman's customers. Begin with those. And Tom . . . especially the garages, you got me?

[CARSON *enters.*

WINSTON'S VOICE

We're on it, Jess . . .

[BARD *switches off the radio.*

CARSON *(holding out letter)*

This, my friend, was brought into the city police station during the noon hour.

BARD *(taking the letter)*

Noon!

CARSON

A bellhop's given six different descriptions of the man who
tipped him five bucks to deliver it. All we know for sure
is the man had two arms, two legs and presumably one
head.

BARD *(takes letter out of envelope, glances at it)*
It's not signed.

CARSON

Go ahead, read it . . . you'll understand why.

BARD *(begins to read briskly . . . and tone changes to a
hushed whisper)*
"To the Police . . . innocent people will be in the house
or automobile with the three fugitives you want. If you
shoot, you will be responsible for taking the lives of
people who have done no harm. Any attempt to trace this
letter will only endanger my family . . . " *(Pause.* BARD
holds letter up to light.) Handwriting disguised . . . no
watermarks.

FREDERICKS

It's a blind.

BARD *(whisper . . . touched)*
The idiot.

CARSON

That letter's no blind.

BARD

But he ought to *know!* God, doesn't he know? Carson, isn't
there some way to get word to this guy, whoever he is,
that you can't play ball with savages like that?

CARSON

How? Without tipping them he wrote that?

BARD

You take a shot in the dark, Federal man! They'll tear

that poor guy to ribbons, inside and out, before they're done. *(Moves down Right.)* You can't co-operate with scum like that!

CARSON

No? . . . What would *you* do, Jesse? I'd say he was smart to write that. Might keep some itchy-fingered officer from shooting his wife or child.

BARD *(whirls)*

Itchy-fingered like me, Carson?

CARSON

You got more sense. That's what's eating you, friend. You know what a spot the man's on. What *would* you do, Jesse . . . under the circumstances?

BARD *(after a moment)*

I'd play ball. (BARD *crosses to desk, flips on intercom and speaks into it.)* Dutch, get me car nine . . . Deputy Winston. *(Flips off the intercom. Quietly.)* Yeah, I reckon I'd do just that. An' maybe pray a little.

WINSTON'S VOICE

Car nine . . .

BARD

Tom . . . stop 'em up there.

WINSTON'S VOICE *(incredulously)*

Stop 'em . . . . ?

BARD

You heard me. I'm countermanding the orders. Bury those prowl cars, *bury* 'em.

FREDERICKS *(angrily)*

You can't put off a showdown, lad.

BARD

Nobody wants a showdown any more'n I do . . . but not

if it means getting some poor slob's family massacred!
(Into mike.) You hear me, Tom? Keep those patrols off
the streets! Stash 'em!

WINSTON'S VOICE

You're callin' it, Jess . . . Listen—that sporty little
foreign car I reported a while ago . . . he just went by the
corner again.

BARD *(considers a moment)*

Okay. Bring him in, Tom. Who knows? But quiet up
there! No sirens, no red lights.

WINSTON'S VOICE

It'll be a pleasure to arrest *any*body!

[BARD *switches off the radio.*

FREDERICKS

You call that police work?

BARD

What do you propose . . . alert 'em, force their hand?

FREDERICKS

That letter pretty well establishes they're in that neighborhood. I'll tell you what I propose—tear gas.

BARD

Anybody wonder why this guy didn't sign his name?
Why he doesn't trust the police to help him?

FREDERICKS

Tear gas and riot guns. I'll have some moved up there
. . . . just in case you begin to see the light!

[FREDERICKS *exits. Pause.*

CARSON *(quietly)*

Changing your tune, Jess? . . .

[BARD *moves to the desk, puzzled at himself and his feelings, ignores Carson. He rereads the letter in silence.*

BARD
Those guys wouldn't try to use a sports car for a getaway. Probably some fresh kid out trying to pick up a girl . . .

(BLACKOUT)

HILLIARD HOME

GLENN *has opened the front door slightly and is looking out through crack, carefully.* HANK *stands behind him, looking out window.* ROBISH *has moved to the steps and stands facing front door.* CINDY *now stands up of sofa, facing Right.* DAN *remains down of Left end of sofa, facing Right. In the bedroom,* ELEANOR *is looking out the window.* RALPHIE *remains on bed, back to audience.*

HANK
He knows something's up . . .

CINDY
Chuck knows nothing. Naturally, he's puzzled . . . he . . .

GLENN *(closes and locks the door)*
Knock off, I'm thinkin'.

HANK
Glenn . . .

GLENN *(abstracted)*
Don't let it get you, kid.

HANK
Glenn . . . I've had it.

GLENN
What're you talkin' about?

HANK

The old man with the trash . . . the teacher . . . now
this guy goin' by out there . . . over'n over. I've had it.

[*Abruptly* HANK *turns and, crossing downstage of Dan,
moves to dining room door.* GLENN *springs after him.*

GLENN

Hey! *(At dining-room door he catches Hank, whips him
about roughly.)* What the hell does that mean? "I've had
it"?

HANK

What're we waitin' for, Glenn?

GLENN

Don't start that again! I gotta dope this . . .

HANK

We're accessories now.

GLENN *(turns to glance at Dan)*

You're learnin' big words aroun' this house, ain't you?

HANK

Glenn . . . I ain't going to the chair 'cause that ape in
there got trigger happy.

GLENN

We're pullin' stakes tomorrow . . . *after* we get the
dough.

HANK *(shouting)*

What good's the dough gonna do you in the death house?

GLENN *(intensely)*

I gotta pay Flick to take care of Bard, don't I? *(Turns,
following* HANK's *gaze, sees Dan.)* What're you gapin' at?

HANK

I'm goin', Glenn. By myself.

GLENN *(whirling on him)*
    You leave here without me, they'll have you back'n stir'n
    less'n a hour.

HANK
    I can take care of myself.

GLENN
    Since when?

HANK *(firmly)*
    Since right now!

    [GLENN *is baffled, angry, frightened, unable to cope.*

GLENN
    Listen, you yellow little punk . . . you're gonna do what
    I tell you!

HANK
    Not any more, Glenn.

DAN *(takes a step to Left)*
    Hank, I don't advise your leaving here alone . . .

HANK
    They won't catch me, Mr. Hilliard. Don't worry about
    that.

GLENN *(wildly)*
    Look who's tellin' who not to worry! You're talkin' like
    Hilliard was our old man. *(Faces Dan.)* If Hilliard was
    our old man, he'd have something coming to him from
    way back! (HANK *turns doorknob and* GLENN *whips about
    . . . changing: pleading now, helpless, slightly pathetic.)*
    Listen, Hank . . . you can't duck out on me. Christ, kid
    . . . it's always been *us.* You'n me. Listen . . . without
    you . . . without you . . .

HANK
    Come along, Glenn?

GLENN *(wildly)*
  Goddammit, I'm callin' the tune! You're gonna listen to
  me, I took care of you, I . . .

  [GLENN *breaks off because* HANK *has taken the automatic from his pocket.* GLENN *stares.*

HANK
  You ain't stoppin' me . . . either one of you. *(Pause.)*
  I'll take the girl's coop.

CINDY *(quickly)*
  They could trace my license in ten minutes.

HANK
  Okay, okay, Miss . . . I can pick up a car anywhere.

  [HANK *stands looking at Cindy, the naked longing clear
  on his face.* GLENN *turns, looks at Cindy, then taps his
  forehead with the heel of his hand.*

GLENN
  I get it. Christ, kid, I get it now! *(He grabs* CINDY *and
  pulls her toward* HANK. DAN *puts his arm around her, holding* GLENN *off.)* Ain't I always learned you? You want
  something, *take* it!

DAN
  Your brother knows it's not that simple, Griffin!

GLENN *(fiercely)*
  I'll *make* it that simple! Hank gets what he wants!

  [*Slight pause.*

HANK *(in choked tones)*
  I doubt it, Glenn. I doubt if I ever will.

  [*Abruptly* HANK *turns and goes out, slamming the door.
  It takes a moment for this to reach* GLENN, *then he whips
  open dining-room door and follows.* ROBISH *moves toward*

front door. As he reaches up Center, the rear door of house is heard to close, off-stage Left. Then ROBISH *continues to front door, opens it slightly, looks out.* ELEANOR, *in bedroom, crosses to door, opens it.*

ELEANOR
Dan . . . ?

DAN
It's all right, Ellie. Where's Ralphie?

ELEANOR
He's here—with me.

[*The dining-room door opens and* GLENN *enters; he looks defeated, haggard, as he sags in dining-room door.* DAN *and* CINDY *turn to him.*

GLENN *(softly)*
He better take care-a himself. Nothin' better happen to . . . *(Then he feels their eyes on him and lofts his chin.)* Good riddance. He was beginnin' to get on my nerves. *(Then suddenly fierce, he steps toward Cindy.)* You satisfied, redhead?

DAN
Cindy had nothing to do with . . .

GLENN *(wild)*
Satisfied?

DAN
Go to your room, Cindy. *(As* GLENN *moves down Right, seething, growing more and more violent,* CINDY *goes to steps.)* Griffin, you'd better get hold of yourself.

ELEANOR *(at bedroom door)* Dan, what is it? What . . .

GLENN *(whirls about and crosses to Left end of sofa)*
All of you, all of you! (With a sudden movement he sweets

everything from end table to Left of sofa; it crashes to floor; GLENN *is breathing hard. He faces Dan.)* You satisfied now, you smart-eyed bastard? Clickety-click, you got at him, didn't you?

DAN *(steps to Glenn)*
God, boy, you'd better . . .

GLENN
Shut up, Pop! . . . Pop! If you was our pop . . .

DAN
Griffin, I don't know how much reason you've got left in that head of yours, but you can't turn this on . . .

GLENN *(pacing down Right like a maddened caged animal)*
I can do anything I want! You and your goddam house!

ROBISH *(at window)*
Stir-crazy!

GLENN
That goddam spitfire'n her fancy skirts swishin'!

DAN
I'd advise you to let loose of that idea!

GLENN *(grabs composition book from sofa)*
That brat an' his "composition"! *(Crosses to Left Center to face Dan again.)*

DAN
If you don't get hold . . .

GLENN
I got hold! I got hold good! *(Twisting the composition book in his hands.)* Now I'm gonna "advise" you, Pop. You're gonna go up there now an' you're gonna learn that kid we ain't playin' cowboys-an'-Indians aroun' here. *(Taking pleasure in it.)* You're gonna give that brat a real old-fashioned lacin'.

DAN

We don't do things that way in this house!

GLENN

This house, this house! I got my gut-full-a this house! *(Eyes on Dan.)* Robish! How'd *you* like to show Hilliard how it's done?

ROBISH *(closes door)*

Yeah . . . I ain't got nothin' else to do.

GLENN *(backing down Right, motioning to Robish)*

Okay, Robish . . . whale the tar outta that brat!

[ROBISH *moves slowly toward steps.*

ROBISH

Little car ain't goin' by out there no more, anyways . . .

[*Quickly* DAN *moves to steps, cuts off* ROBISH. DAN *meets* ELEANOR; *she steps aside along Right in hall.* ROBISH *stops.* DAN *opens bedroom door, enters.* RALPHIE *rises and faces him in bedroom.*

GLENN

Let's hear him bawlin', Pop. Loud. My old man used a belt!

[DAN *stands with his back against door, looking at* Ralphie. ELEANOR *leans across bannister.*

ELEANOR *(To Glenn)*

I hope they get your brother. I hope they kill him!

GLENN

That happens, lady . . . you all get it. *(Lifts voice.)* We don't hear nothin', Hilliard!

DAN *(breathlessly)*

Ralphie . . .

RALPHIE

Did Hank take your gun? Then there's only one gun now . . .

DAN *(gently, but urgently)*

Son . . . you've got to help . . .

ROBISH *(on steps)*

What's goin' on in there, Hilliard?

DAN *(swiftly, softly, suffering)*

Ralphie . . . listen to me. No matter what you think now . . . no matter what you think of me . . . what names you give it . . . you've got to do what I tell you.

ROBISH *(steps to door)*

What's the stall?

DAN

Ralphie, listen! I want you to cry. *(Almost a whisper.)* Do you hear me? Ralphie . . . son . . . please . . . for God's sake do what I say now.

RALPHIE

I . . . I can't.

ROBISH *(outside the door)*

You want some help, Hilliard?

[*Trapped,* DAN *lifts his hand and brings it down, in desperation, open-palmed: a stinging blow across the boy's face.* RALPHIE, *stunned, stands staring at his father.* DAN *goes sick and empty clear through. Then* DAN *sinks to his knees, gathers* RALPHIE *in his arms, and* RALPHIE *begins to cry. He cries softly at first, then louder and louder.* GLENN *hears the sounds and drops the composition book to the floor, as though he has found some small release inside.* ELEANOR *turns to Cindy, fighting tears.*

(DIMOUT)

SHERIFF'S OFFICE

Clock reads 8:59. WINSTON *stands to Left of* CHUCK, *who, bewildered, faces* BARD *seated at desk,* BARD *is examining* CHUCK'S *driver's license.*

BARD

What's your business, Mr. . . . *(Glances at license.)* Wright?

CHUCK

Attorney, Swisshelm and Edwards. Circle Tower Building . . . What's this all about?

BARD

Your firm handle criminal cases?

CHUCK

We're strictly corporation law. You haven't answered my question, Deputy.

WINSTON

Don't get fresh.

BARD

Empty out your pockets, Wright.

CHUCK

You've no right to . . .

BARD

Look, Wright . . . you're not in court! Empty out your pockets! *(As* CHUCK *complies.)* What you been up to, last hour or so . . . in that . . . *(Consults Chuck's registration.)* Jaguar of yours? Cruising round in circles?

WINSTON

You scoutin' for those rats, Wright?

CHUCK

What rats?

BARD

Let's not be cagey, kid . . . it makes me suspicious.
(Picks up newspaper from desk and hands it to CHUCK,
who reads the headlines and begins to realize . . .) We
know they're up there somewhere . . . holed up in one
of those nice houses . . . so . . . *(Stops, frowning . . .
studying expression on* CHUCK's *face.)* What's up, boy?

CHUCK

Nothing . . .

BARD

You know something?
(When CHUCK *shakes his head.)* Suspect something?

CHUCK

No . . .

BARD *(rising)*

Dammit, don't lie to me! Your face looks like I just
kicked you.

CHUCK

Well . . . it's just that . . . my girl lives . . . there.

BARD

Name?

CHUCK

Her name's . . . Allen. *(Firmly.)* Constance Allen.

WINSTON *(consulting the list)*

No Allens on the list, Jess.

BARD *(picks up Dan's letter, hands it to Chuck)*

Here . . . read this. (BARD *sits as* CHUCK *reads.)* Now.
Let's have it, kid. What's the girl's name?

CHUCK

I . . . don't know.

BARD *(gently probing now)*

She's in there . . . with those three. What's the address?

CHUCK

If . . . if he'd wanted you to know . . . *(Tosses letter to the desk.)* he'd have signed his name.

BARD *(changing)*

Wright, that guy ought to know he can't cribbage aroun' with the police like this. If he doesn't, you should!

CHUCK

What do you expect him to do? He's doing all he can! He's quite a guy!

BARD *(rising)*

Kid . . . I honestly don't know what I'd do if I was in your shoes . . . but I'm in mine . . . and I want that name. Now spit it out or I'll slap you in the pokey so fast . . .

CHUCK

You've got no charges!

BARD

I've got sixty of 'em. Aidin' and abettin' . . . withholding evidence . . . accessory to murder! Or didn't you know they murdered a man this afternoon? Yeah, that's the kind of scum you're lettin' your girl spend the evening with.

[*Pause.* CHUCK *crosses and sinks into chair at Left.* BARD *sits on edge of desk.* CHUCK *swallows.*

CHUCK

I . . . I can't make that decision. For them. You'd better slap on one of those charges, Deputy. Because I don't know the name. I never said I did.

BARD *(rising)*
Why, you young . . . *(He is interrupted by the intercom.)*

DUTCH'S VOICE
Special Agent Carson, Jesse.

BARD *(switches on radio)*
Yes, Carson?

CARSON'S VOICE
Deputy . . . it just blew wide open!

BARD
What? . . . What've you got?

CARSON'S VOICE
City policemen just caught Hank Griffin trying to steal a car. He decided to shoot it out . . .

BARD
Killed?

CARSON'S VOICE
Killed.

[*Pause.*

BARD *(in a different tone . . . very quietly)*
Anything else?

CARSON'S VOICE
Plenty . . . The gun the boy was carrying—it was registered. *(As* BARD'S *eyes meet* CHUCK'S.) In the name of Hilliard . . . Daniel C. Hilliard.

[BARD *glances at* WINSTON, *who glances at list, looks up, nods.*

BARD
    Just like that. Eleanor Hilliard wrote a check to Claude
    Patterson this morning.

WINSTON *(reading from list)*
    Hilliard, Daniel C. Wife, Eleanor. One son age ten, Ralph.
    One daughter age twenty, Cynthia . . . called Cindy.

    [CHUCK *is watching* WINSTON. *Their eyes now meet.*

BARD *(after a slight pause—into radio)*
    Okay. Carson . . . throw a cordon around the Hilliard
    house. Let no one in or out of that block. Only keep every-
    thing out of sight of the windows. I'll be up there in ten
    minutes. And Carson . . . have the newsboys got this?

CARSON'S VOICE
    Not yet. Not even the death.

BARD
    Well, for God's sake, keep 'em off it!

CARSON'S VOICE
    We'll try, Jess.

    [BARD *flips off the radio.*

WINSTON *(gets coat)*
    You call it, Jess.

CHUCK *(rising)*
    You can't move in! You read Mr. Hilliard's letter.

BARD *(taking his revolver out of desk drawer, checks it.
    Abstracted)*
    Get out of here now, kid.

CHUCK *(demanding)*
    What're you going to do?

BARD

> What the sweet hell do you think I'm going to do . . . blow up the house?

[BARD *takes his jacket from back of chair and starts putting it on.*

CHUCK *(earnestly—crossing to Bard)*

> Deputy . . . what if you could sneak someone inside? With a gun. There are only two of them in there now.

WINSTON *(putting on coat—at Left)*

> This is police work, son. Stay out of it. *(Goes off Left.)*

CHUCK

> If somebody was in there . . . between them and the family . . . and if he could get 'em both at one crack . . .

BARD *(to Chuck)*

> Don't get any wild ideas. Anything goes haywire now— cause you want to play Boy Scout—that girl'll never forgive you. *(Into intercom.)* Dutch! Get an ambulance up to Kessler and Keystone. Keep it out of sight. *(Flips off intercom.)*

CHUCK *(helplessly; urgently)*

> But what can I *do?*

BARD

> You can hightail it out of here . . . maybe say a prayer. Nothing else, hear? *Nothing!*

CHUCK *(grabbing Bard)*

> What are *you* going to do?

BARD *(annoyed—because he doesn't have the answer)*

> Will you get out of here!

[WINSTON *appears with rifle.* CHUCK *turns, sees this . . . his face sets . . . and he makes up his mind, walks out.*

WINSTON
  The boy's got a good question, Jess.

BARD *(thoughtfully; quietly)*
  A damn good question . . . I wish I had the answer.
  (Then briskly, as he starts out with WINSTON *following.)*
  Well, let's get on it now. Let's get up there.

DIMOUT

CURTAIN

THE DESPERATE HOURS

ACT THREE

ACT THREE

HILLIARD HOME

DAN *is at window of master bedroom.* ELEANOR *sitting on edge of bed.* RALPHIE *sleeps on bed.* CINDY *is out of view— in her own room. In the living room* ROBISH *is at front window, looking out, alert, frowning, suspicious. As the curtain rises, he calls.*

ROBISH
Griffin! *(Slightly louder.)* Griffin! (GLENN *enters from dining room.)* Griffin . . . somethin' funny goin' on. There ain't been no cars go by out there for a long time. (GLENN *has paused down Left;* ROBISH *takes a step from window, staring at Glenn.)* Griffin, you deef?

[*A change has come over* GLENN; *he seems abstracted, his face blank, his eyes staring; he is on the verge of cracking up and he is not quite "in touch" with the reality around him. Beneath this exterior, we feel there is a dynamic danger even worse than before. When he enters, he moves down Left, pacing—a wildness in him.*

GLENN
Robish . . . let's grab the two women'n blow.

ROBISH
With no dough?

GLENN *(vacantly)*
With no dough.

ROBISH
Okay. Ya wanna go . . . go. Wind up like the kid brother. In the morgue.

145

GLENN *(steps toward Center)*
Lay off, Robish.

ROBISH
On a slab. By this time they got 'im or shot 'im.

[*Above,* DAN *goes to bedroom door.*

GLENN *(wildly)*
Nothin' happens to Hank!

ROBISH *(chuckles heavily)*
That's po'try, Griffin. Got 'im or shot 'im.

GLENN *(starting toward Robish)*
You don't know nothin'! Goddam you, Robish . . .

[ROBISH *lifts the gun, almost casually. In this moment, the telephone shrills.* GLENN *stops down Center.*

ROBISH *(shouting)*
Hilliard! Answer that!

[DAN *opens the door, and picks up the phone in the hall at the time that* GLENN, *below, is already answering it.* CINDY *has come out of her room and stands near the door to Ralphie's room.* DAN, *undecided as to what to do with the phone, looks at Cindy.*

GLENN *(leaping to the phone almost before the first ring is over)*
Hank! *(Into instrument.)* Hello! *(Then, sagging in disappointment, snarls.)* Who? . . . *(He replaces the phone angrily.)*

ROBISH *(approaching Glenn)*
Christ, *who is it?*

GLENN *(vacantly, going through dining-room door)*
Something about . . . a night watchman . . . *(Exits.)*

ROBISH *(calling)*
Hilliard!

DAN *(speaks into the extension)*
Hello . . . this is Mr. Hilliard speaking. *(Suddenly alert.)* Yes, Carl? . . . I'll be right down. (DAN *replaces phone and turns.*

ROBISH *(at steps)*
Who was that? What's going on?

DAN
The money's here. It arrived special delivery at the store. I'll go get it.

[DAN *turns and enters the bedroom, where he faces* ELEANOR, *who is sitting on the bed.* CINDY *returns to her own room.* GLENN *has returned from the dining room during Dan's last speech.* ROBISH *turns to him.*

ROBISH *(trying to penetrate Glenn's preoccupation)*
Griffin . . . the dough's here.

GLENN *(stands for a moment at dining-room door)*
How come that wasn't Hank on the phone?

ROBISH
You better snap out of it. *(As* GLENN *goes into the den.)* Jeez, you're givin' me the willies . . .

[*He stands looking after* GLENN. *In the bedroom above,* DAN *picks up his coat from bed and paces with the coat in his hands.* ELEANOR *follows him with her eyes as she speaks.*

ELEANOR
I can't believe it. Now. Tonight! No more waiting. In an hour now . . . *Less* than an hour! *(Slight pause.* DAN *puts on his coat.)* Dan . . . look at me . . . *(Rises, fighting alarm.)* Dan!

ROBISH *(shouting as he crosses to window at Right)* Hilliard! That dough's waiting!

ELEANOR

Tell me. What are you planning, Dan?

[*Pause.* DAN *turns to face her.*

DAN

I can't wait any longer for the opportune moment, that's all.

ELEANOR

What do you mean?

DAN

I've got to . . . make the moment . . . for myself.

ELEANOR

Dan, tell me. My blood's stopped. Dan . . .

DAN

There are only three bullets left in that gun down there.

ELEANOR

I'm going to scream!

DAN

No you're not, you're going to listen.

ELEANOR

My heart's pushing up out of . . . Dan, *what do you mean?*

DAN

I'm going to force Robish to use those bullets.

ELEANOR *(whispers)*

Use them . . . How?

DAN *(quietly)*

On me.

ROBISH *(crosses to up Center)*

Hilliard, what's the stall?

ELEANOR *(rising, to him)*
> Dan, this isn't you. They've driven you . . . Oh, God, *Dan!*

DAN
> I've tried every other way, haven't I? *Haven't* I?

ELEANOR *(swiftly . . . in a whisper)*
> We know, we're not asking for more, we know what you've done. Even Ralphie . . .

DAN
> If I can get Griffin out of the way before Robish even knows what's happening . . . *(Grimly; murderously)* And I *can.*

ELEANOR
> Dan, no matter how much you want to kill Griffin . . .

DAN
> There's no other way!

ELEANOR
> There *is.* There has to be!

DAN *(gently, urgently)*
> Darling, you've got to face this with me. Griffin hates me. He hated me before he even saw me. I can't explain it. Every hour some new black hole appears in him. He's cracking up, Ellie. God knows what a mind like that will turn to . . . which one of us . . . Now. Do you see? We're no better off when I get the money. Do you see?

ELEANOR
> All I see is one thing. One thing . . . We're not saved if *you* die.

DAN *(turns away)*
> Please, Ellie, don't make it so . . .

ELEANOR
> All right . . . go down there. Kill Griffin. Make Robish
> shoot you. Do you imagine a man like that has to have
> *bullets* to . . . (DAN *turns to her.*) against Ralphie?
> . . . or Cindy? . . . or me? *Do* you?

DAN *(realizing that it was only panic, softly)*
> All right, Ellie.

ELEANOR
> We're not saved if you die.

DAN
> All *right*, Ellie!

ELEANOR *(sits on bed)*
> Oh, God, darling. Dan . . . you're the hub . . . it all
> revolves around you. If anything . . .

DAN
> Everything's blurred again. One minute it all looks sharp
> . . . clear . . .

ELEANOR *(places her hand on Dan's)*
> Dan. *(He looks at her.)* We can't let them panic us now.

[*There is a moment of understanding between them.*

ROBISH *(moves to steps)*
> Hilliard! Get th' lead out!

[DAN *and* ELEANOR *break.* DAN *turns and opens door.*
ELEANOR *moves to door and stands there.* CINDY *enters
hall from her room.* DAN *goes down steps.* ROBISH *moves
to Left, gun in hand.*

ROBISH
> Goddam you, Hilliard, if you think . . .

[GLENN *enters from den; he moves swiftly, like a caged
animal. He is wild, as before, crossing to upstage of sofa.*

GLENN

Ask 'em where they get the news on that damn thing!
(Sinks to chair down Right.)

ROBISH *(as* DAN *pauses at steps)*
We ain't gonna blow till we get that dough, Hilliard!

GLENN
Where's the redhead?

[DAN *turns to* CINDY, *who is in hall.*

DAN
Cindy, go to your room. Lock the door.

GLENN
Redhead goes along!

[CINDY *remains in hall.*

ROBISH *(turning to Glenn)*
The gal stays right here.

GLENN *(ignoring Robish—a grotesque caricature of his old
self)*
Open the letter . . . take out two thousand dollars . . .

ROBISH *(one step toward Center)*
To hell with that!

GLENN
Redhead takes it to Lombardi's Grille . . .

DAN *(putting on coat)*
Cindy is not going to deliver any . . .

GLENN *(turns in chair to face Dan)*
Lombardi Grille. South Illinois Street.

ROBISH
To hell with that. Ain't got time now!

GLENN

She sits'n has a drink. A man sits down with her. Then . . .

ROBISH

Then nothin'! Yuh lissen to me . . .

GLENN *(vaguely)*

Then . . .

DAN *(crosses to upstage of sofa)*

What then, Griffin?

GLENN

She gives him the dough. Two G's.

[DAN *turns and nods to* CINDY *who comes down steps and crosses to front door.*

ROBISH

Yuh bring all that dough here, Hilliard . . . soon's yuh lay your mitts on it

[DAN *goes to open the front door.*

GLENN

We don't get outta here till I hear from Flick he's got his money.

[DAN, *with door open, now nods to* CINDY, *who goes out.* DAN *follows and closes the door.* GLENN *rises and crosses downstage of sofa to Left.*

ROBISH *(crossing to front door, locks it)*

Now, how we gonna take two dames in the car? *(He locks the door as* GLENN *goes to the phone, dials.)* Loco. Christ! Loco.

[ROBISH *goes toward dining room door.*

GLENN *(on phone)*

What? . . . Oh . . . Mr. Flick. Room . . . uh . . . 202.

ROBISH *(turns. In dining-room door)*
I lay my hands'n that dough, yuh can rot'n here Griffin.
(Exits.)

(BLACKOUT)

THE WALLINGS' ATTIC

The corner of an attic room that seems to be suspended in darkness. The room has a cluttered look: discarded furniture, an old iron bed-frame leaning against the wall. A single small window overlooks the Hilliard house in the distance. CARSON is looking out the window through binoculars. BARD behind him, wearing hat. FREDERICKS is seated on an old trunk. On an old box at Right is radio apparatus. A rifle with a telescopic sight leans against the wall near the window.

CARSON *(reporting, without lowering binoculars)*
Jesse . . . a man and a girl just came out the front door of the Hilliard house.

BARD
That'll be Hilliard and his daughter.

CARSON
They're getting into the black coupé in the driveway. *(He hands the glasses to BARD, who looks through the window.)* Cocky, aren't they? Letting them both out of there even now.

BARD
Yeah . . . gettin' real cocksure.

FREDERICKS *(crisply)*
Why not? They know they got us hog-tied . . . 's long as we sit up here in the attic of the house next door.

BARD *(hands glasses back to Carson and turns to Fredericks)*
Don't start riding me again, Fredericks.

[There is a buzz from the radio apparatus. BARD *stops, flips a switch and picks up the microphone.*

WINSTON'S VOICE *(on radio)*
Car nine—Winston.

BARD *(into mike)*
Yeah, Tom?

WINSTON'S VOICE
Jesse . . . Hilliard and his daughter just turned south on Keystone. You want me to pick 'em up?

BARD
No.

FREDERICKS
What the hell're we waitin' for? We got the phone tap. We know where he's going.

BARD *(annoyed—into mike)*
Tom . . . let them get downtown to that store. Then . . . when he's got his mail, whatever it is . . . pick him up and bring him here to the Wallings' house. Come in here from the north, though . . . and careful nobody in the Hilliard windows can see you.

WINSTON'S VOICE
What'll I tell the guy?

BARD
Nothing. *(Flips off radio, puts down mike.)*

FREDERICKS
Bard, this is stupid as hell! We can't cool our heels up here in this attic all night! I tell you, we got no choice now. Move in!

BARD

And I tell you I've got an animal gnawing away inside me tonight, Fredericks, and I don't need this crap from you! I'm aware of the alternatives. We could bust in there now . . . or try to bluff 'em out . . . or try to sneak in and flush 'em . . . but . . .

FREDERICKS *(rising)*

Let's get one thing straight. There's going to be blood. There're only two people in that house now.

BARD

Two human beings.

FREDERICKS

Okay! Measure them against the just as innocent people those two can knock off if they bluff their way out of this trap.

BARD

The guy's wife and kid!

FREDERICKS

Lad, you're putting a weapon in the hands of every felon in the country, you let . . .

BARD *(overriding)*

I didn't invent the scheme, dammit! I'm doing all I can. We've got sixty officers in those woods now . . . the streets are blocked off . . .

FREDERICKS

Bastards like them're wily.

BARD *(turning to Carson)*

Carson! Those're escapees from a Federal prison in there. You call it!

[*Pause.*

CARSON *(turns from window slightly)*
  I'll string along with you, Deputy . . . at least until we
  speak to Hilliard.

FREDERICKS
  O-kay, lads. It's your baby. I'm just a sour old man hates
  to see frisky young slobs make fools of theirselves. *(Harshly.)* But pity's a luxury your badge don't afford!

  [*The radio buzzes.* BARD *flips switch, picks up mike.*

BARD *(into mike)*
  Deputy Bard . . .

DUTCH'S VOICE
  We just got another telephone report, Jess. A man's voice,
  unidentified, *inside* the house called a downtown hotel
  . . . spoke to a man named Flick . . . told him to meet
  a red-headed girl at Lombardi Grille . . . South Illinois
  Street.

BARD *(lowers mike)*
  God Almighty, that's the daughter. *(Into mike.)* Dutch
  . . . put a city detective in the Lombardi Grille. Have
  him pick up the man and the girl.

DUTCH'S VOICE
  There's more. The one called Flick is supposed to call
  back to the Hilliard house . . . let the telephone ring
  three times, then hang up. Some sort of hanky-panky.

BARD
  Thanks, Dutch. *(Flips off radio. Puts down mike.)* Wonder what the devil that's all about.

CARSON *(quietly—looking through the glasses)*
  Bard . . . there's some sort of activity behind the Hilliard garage. You can barely make it out in the light from
  the window.

BARD *(takes glasses, looks)*
Looks to me like somebody stretched out on the ground

FREDERICKS
Let's get over there!

BARD
Whoever it is, he's heading for that porch.

CARSON
Shall we give the signal to close in, Jess?

BARD
He's climbing up . . .

(BLACKOUT)

HILLIARD HOME

The house is dimmer than before. ELEANOR *and* RALPHIE
stand at window of master bedroom, backs to audience.
ROBISH *is not in view.* GLENN *is seated on sofa, listening to
newscast on small portable radio. Through the following the*
RADIO NEWSCASTER'S VOICE *is heard indistinctly under
Robish's lines.*

RADIO NEWSCASTER *(on speaker, under scene)*
. . . see what the weather man has in store for us. Clear
skies tomorrow. Much colder, with brisk winds tomorrow
and Sunday. No more rain is predicted for the Indianapolis
area . . . but better dig out that overcoat because winter
is almost here! . . . This has been your ten o'clock news.
Next newscast at eleven-thirty; important bulletins will
be broadcast as they are received. Kyle McGreevey saying Good Night and Good Cheer!

[*Through the above speech,* ROBISH's *voice is heard off Left.*

ROBISH'S VOICE

Griffin! *(Louder.)* Griffin! *(As* GLENN *makes a gesture to silence Robish.* ROBISH *appears in dining-room door; he is terrified.)* Can't yuh hear me? *(Crosses to front door.)* Lissen! I seen somethin' movin' out by the garage! *(Opens door a crack and looks out, gun ready.)* Hey, out there! Anybody out there? *(Turns uncertainly.)* Griffin! (GLENN *doesn't stir;* ROBISH *is bewildered, lost without his "leader"; he turns to door again.)* Lissen, anybody out there— coppers! We'll blast the woman and kid in here! *(He closes door, locks it, turns to Glenn.)* Griffin, yuh hear me?

[*At end of newscast,* GLENN *snaps off radio—jubilant. There is a growing wildness in him. Convinced now, deluding himself into thinking what he wants to believe, he enters another phase—in which nothing can touch him. This is in sharp contrast to the stunned, glassy fear of the last scenes. He is gay, refusing reality, like a man with too many drinks. He rises, snaps fingers happily.*

GLENN

He's okay!

ROBISH

Griffin, I seen somethin' out there—

GLENN *(mounting joy as he crosses to Left chair)*
Hank's okay, Robish! *(Sits.)*

ROBISH *(moves to Glenn, so that his back is to the steps and the hall)*
To hell with the kid, he's in the clink.

[CHUCK *cautiously opens the door of Cindy's room, looks out, a gun in his hand.*

GLENN

They'd have had it on the news, wouldn't they? (CHUCK *moves carefully down hall toward Ralphie's bedroom.*) Nothin'! They're still lookin' for *all* of us! Not a goddam word about Hank!

ROBISH

Lissen, we gotta change our ideas!

GLENN *(rises—turns—as* CHUCK *lets himself into Ralphie's bedroom)*

Idea's perkin' fine. Everythin's chimin'. *Hank made it!* He's on his way to Helen!

[CHUCK *half-closes Ralphie's door and* GLENN *strides down Center.*

ROBISH *(disgusted)*

Who yuh tryin' to con? I tell yuh, I seen somethin' move out by the garage. *(Crosses to dining-room door.)*

GLENN *(high spirits. Laughs—moves down Right)*

Goblins, Robish. Like on Halloween when we was kids. God, how Hank used to go for that Halloween crap! Dress up . . . burnt cork'n his face . . .

ROBISH

Them's coppers out there.

GLENN

We're snug, we're snug. Two hours now, we'll be in Louisville. Hank's with Helen.

ROBISH *(in dining-room door)*

They put that on the radio, did they? Any cops stick their necks 'n here, I blow up the whole goddam house.

[CHUCK *is now in Ralphie's bedroom, his gun ready and* ROBISH *exits into dining room.*

(BLACKOUT)

THE WALLINGS' ATTIC

FREDERICKS *is seated on the trunk.* BARD *has the glasses and is looking out the window.* CARSON *stands by.*

FREDERICKS

If there's any shooting over there . . .

BARD *(hands glasses to Carson, turns)*

I'll give the signal to close in. Satisfied, Lieutenant?

FREDERICKS *(rises as* CARSON *takes up the watch through the window)*

No, I'm not. There's another gun in that house now . . . 'cause we waited.

BARD *(moves down Right)*

What I'd like to know is how that kid got through the police lines.

FREDERICKS

Plenty of ways . . . you know the neighborhood well enough.

CARSON *(his first show of emotion)*

A reckless muddlehead like that could botch up everything if he startles them in there!

FREDERICKS

Why shouldn't he take it in his own hands?

CARSON

If only his gun's between those two and the family somehow . . .

BARD

My hunch is the boy's layin' low . . . not knowin' where everybody is . . . waitin' for someone to make a move . . . us or them.

FREDERICKS
Lads, you're up a creek.

CARSON
The boy's smart enough to know he's done for if he doesn't get them both at the same time . . . and fast!

FREDERICKS
Lads, you're up a long, long creek and no paddles.

[*The radio buzzes.* BARD *flips switch, picks up mike.*

BARD *(into mike)*
Deputy Bard . . .

WINSTON'S VOICE *(on radio)*
Jess . . . Hilliard's on his way upstairs. Tread easy now, you guys. This gentleman's had it.

[BARD *flips off radio, puts down mike. They all wait, looking up Left.*

FREDERICKS *(as he rises)*
Man plays with dynamite, he's going to get it.

[DAN *enters up Left, looks around, quietly terrified but determined as he moves Center.*

BARD
Evening, Mr. Hilliard. My name's Bard. Deputy Sheriff, Marion County . . . I received your letter, Mr. Hilliard.

DAN
I didn't write you any letter.

BARD *(taking letter out of his pocket)*
Look, Mr. Hilliard . . . we wouldn't be here if we didn't have it all pretty straight. So let's not waste . . . *(Stops, staring into Dan's face; then, very gently.)* Sorry. You want to sit down, Mr. Hilliard?

*[*BARD *helps* DAN *to trunk where he sits, back to audience.*

DAN *(flatly)*
  Where'd I slip up?

BARD
  You didn't. Young Griffin's dead. He had your gun.

DAN *(the name sinking in . . . recognition)*
  Bard . . . Bard . . . do you know a man named Flick?

BARD
  I've heard the name.

DAN
  My daughter's paying Flick two thousand dollars to kill
  you.

BARD
  So . . . *(In wonder.)* So that's the way he was going to
  do it. *(Briskly.)* Well, Mr. Flick's being arrested, right
  about now . . . Lombardi Grille . . .

DAN *(rises, steps threateningly toward Bard)*
  You fool! You damned clumsy . . .

BARD
  Okay, Hilliard. Let off steam. Take a swing. How'd I
  know what they'd send your girl into? I swear . . .

DAN
  Swear? What can you swear to? That when I'm not back
  in there in time . . . when Flick doesn't call . . . they
  won't jump to the conclusion that . . . *(Breaks off.)*
  What can anyone swear to?

BARD
  Don't worry about Flick's call, Mr. Hilliard. We know the
  signal. We can handle it.

DAN *(picks up rifle with telescopic sight)*
    Are you planning to use this?

FREDERICKS
    They both still in there?

DAN
    Yes.

BARD *(takes rifle from Dan, replaces it)*
    How many guns?

DAN *(looks out window toward his own house)*
    One. With three bullets.

FREDERICKS
    That helps!

DAN *(turns to Fredericks. Slowly)*
    Also . . . my wife and son.

FREDERICKS
    Mr. Hilliard—if these two convicts get away with this
    scheme . . .

DAN
    I don't care about that now. I don't want them . . . or
    you . . . to kill my wife or boy. That's first. *First.* God
    help me, that comes first.

BARD
    Noboly's blaming you, Mr. Hilliard. Nobody in his right
    mind can raise a voice against what you've done . . . But
    I can't let you go back in there.

    [*Pause. Then, slowly,* DAN *takes the special delivery en-
    velope containing money from his inside topcoat pocket.
    He hands it to* BARD, *who examines the contents.*

DAN
    Until they get that . . . they're not coming out.

FREDERICKS *(crisply)*
    Then we move in.

DAN *(erupting)*
    What'm I supposed to do . . . *sit up here and watch it
    happen?*

FREDERICKS
    It's plain suicide for you to go back in there now!

DAN
    That may be. There comes a time when that fact just
    doesn't enter in . . . You don't give a hang about a life
    or two . . . what's one more?

BARD *(drops envelope with money on trunk; he is having an
    inner struggle)*
    Mr. Hilliard . . . we're trying to help you.

DAN *(pleading forcefully, hopelessly)*
    Then clear out! Get away. Take your men . . . your
    rifles . . . your floodlights . . . and *get away!*

    [CARSON *steps in, picks up the envelope with the money
    and holds it out to Dan.*

CARSON
    We can't do that, Mr. Hilliard. I'll give you ten minutes
    . . . from the time you walk through that door over
    there. Shortly after you're inside, we'll give them the
    telephone signal they're waiting for. If you need us,
    flicker a light. You've got ten minutes. It's on your
    shoulders.

    [*Pause.* DAN *takes the envelope.* CARSON *steps back.*

BARD
    Mr. Hilliard, you'd better have the whole picture. Charles
    Wright is in the house.

DAN *(amazed. Turns to Bard)*
    Chuck?

BARD
    And he's armed. We couldn't prevent it. *(Slight pause.)*
    Do you want a gun, Mr. Hilliard?

DAN *(quietly)*
    No . . . thanks. *(He puts the envelope into his inside
    topcoat pocket.)*

BARD
    They search you when you come in? (DAN *nods slowly.)*
    Good luck . . . sir.

    [DAN *turns to go . . . then stops . . . turns.*

DAN
    I've changed my mind.

BARD
    You want a gun?

DAN
    Please.

    [BARD *takes his own revolver from his holster and hands
    it to Dan.*

BARD
    You know how to use it?

    [DAN *looks at revolver, nods, breaks it and shakes the
    bullets into his hand, examines the empty chamber.*

FREDERICKS *(shocked)*
    Are you crazy?

DAN
    Maybe. Only a crazy man'd go in there with an empty
    gun. Griffin doesn't think I'm crazy.

BARD
    That's a pretty long shot, isn't it?

DAN
    I don't have any short ones in sight. Do you?

    [DAN *firmly puts the bullets into* BARD'S *hand. Then, he turns and goes down the stairs. Pause. Then* BARD *flips switch on the radio, picks up mike.*

BARD *(into mike)*
    Car nine . . . Winston.

WINSTON'S VOICE Parked in side drive, Jess.
    Tom . . . take Mr. Hilliard back to his car. (BARD *puts down mike, flips off the radio; thoughtfully.)* How'd you like to be riding up to *your* door like that, Fredericks?

FREDERICKS
    Just luck I'm not. Or you.

BARD
    Yeah. They didn't happen to pick on us, that's all.

    [BARD *picks up binoculars from window sill.* CARSON *looks at his watch.*

(BLACKOUT

HILLIARD HOME

    ELEANOR *and* RALPHIE *are in the master bedroom at the window.* CHUCK *still stands in Ralphie's room with the door open, listening, waiting.* GLENN *is in Left chair.* ROBISH *is turning from the front window.* CHUCK *draws back into bedroom.*

ROBISH
    Here he comes, Griffin!

GLENN *(exhilarated; rises)*
> Only two hours, Robish! Two lousy hours. I'll do the drivin', make it in less!

> [DAN *appears on porch, his hands shoved deep into his topcoat pockets.*

ROBISH
> The little gal ain't with him.

> [CHUCK *closes door of bedroom, stays out of sight now.*

GLENN
> Who cares? Who gives a damn?

> [ROBISH *opens front door, closes it after Dan, locks it. DAN moves to up Center, facing GLENN, who steps to him. ROBISH is behind, to Right. GLENN's mood is almost a travesty on his previous behavior. DAN's manner is profoundly quiet, as he sizes up the situation with a glance upstairs, but determined to get and hold Glenn's attention. ELEANOR crosses to bedroom door and RALPHIE joins her.*

ROBISH
> Hand over the dough, Hilliard.

DAN *(ignores this, lifts voice)*
> Stay in there, Ellie. Keep the door locked.

ROBISH
> Yuh hear me?

DAN *(flatly—almost a challenge)*
> I don't have it.

ROBISH *(roaring)*
> What?

GLENN *(steps to Dan)*
> Now, Pop . . . who you kiddin'? Take your hands outta your pockets . . . *please.*

[*This is what* DAN *wants. He does so, facing Glenn.* GLENN *frisks him, feels the gun in the pocket, reaches in.*

ROBISH
I'll take the cash, Griffin.

[GLENN *takes the gun out of Dan's pocket with his right hand, looking into Dan's eyes.*

GLENN
What'd you say, Robish? *(He whips the gun out, points it at Robish and pushes* DAN *around behind him.)* I didn't hear you, Robish!

[ROBISH *stares at the gun, lowering his own.*

ROBISH *(steps toward Dan)*
You lousy sonofa . . .

GLENN *(laughs)*
Had it all doped, didn't you? *(He reaches with his left hand, keeping the aim on Robish, into Dan's inside coat pocket . . . brings out the envelope.)* This is what you had in mind, Robish?

ROBISH *(to Dan)*
You bastard!

GLENN *(stepping toward* ROBISH, *who backs away)*
Not Pop. Not my old pal Pop! *(Pockets the money.)* Any objections, Robish?

ROBISH
Let's get outta here.

[*The telephone rings.* ROBISH *makes a move to answer it.*

GLENN
Stay away from it, Robish. *(They all stand and listen in frozen silence while the phone rings three times: spaced,*

automatic. GLENN *waits after the third ring until he's sure that there won't be a fourth. He laughs.)* Well, that takes care of Bard! Time to break up housekeeping.

ROBISH

Let's get movin'.

DAN *(between Glenn and steps)*

Griffin . . . you'd better take me along. *Only* me!

ROBISH

Like hell. We gotta have a dame in the car!

[GLENN *has stopped, looks at Dan.*

DAN

Griffin . . . I'm the only one who knows you hired a man named Flick to kill Bard.

GLENN *(makes the "clickety-click" gesture)*

Clickety-clickety-click. Right up to the very end!

DAN

You'd better take me along.

GLENN

Nothin' can touch me now, Hilliard! Everythin's goin' my way!

ROBISH *(glancing out front window)*

Come on. Them woods out there could be full-a Feds, all we know.

GLENN

And you . . . you, Hilliard, can come along, too. 'Cause it's like this, see—Hank's waitin'.

DAN

Waiting?

ROBISH

You're off your rocker!

GLENN

So I'm in a kinda hurry! *(With gun he prods* DAN *backwards to Left and goes up the steps.)* Hey, missus, get the brat ready. We're goin' on a little picnic.

[GLENN *reaches for door knob, finds door locked.* ELEANOR *and* RALPHIE *back away from door, to Left.*

ROBISH *(covers Dan with pistol, moves Left)*
He's gettin' some sense back.

[GLENN *pushes on bedroom door, rattling knob.*

GLENN

Hey, folks, you don't wanna miss the fun, the ice cream'll all be et up.

[DAN *takes a step toward the hall, but* ROBISH, *with gun lifted, steps toward Dan and moves to Left, with* DAN *backing up toward dining room door.* CHUCK *edges open the door of Ralphie's bedroom; he now stands behind* GLENN, *who is knocking on bedroom door.*

ROBISH *(to Dan)*
Where yuh think you're goin'?

GLENN

Lady, you don't want me to have to kick in that nice shiny door, do you?

[GLENN *steps back, lifts his leg, kicks the door; it splinters.* CHUCK *lifts his gun, as* GLENN *starts to kick a second time, and brings it down with great force behind Glenn's ear;* GLENN, *caught off balance, falls back into the hall, momentarily unconscious.*

ROBISH

No noise, Griffin! No . . .

[ROBISH *turns and sees* CHUCK, *who comes down the*

steps. ROBISH *fires, hitting* CHUCK, *whose gun explodes toward the floor as he falls forward upstage of sofa.* ROBISH, *unthinking, dashes downstage of sofa toward front door.* ELEANOR, *hearing the shots, cries out, running to the door without opening it.*

ELEANOR
  Dan!

DAN *(shouting)*
  Stay there, Ellie!

  [ROBISH *has opened front door slightly; a flood light illuminates the house from off Right.*

ROBISH
  Hey, out there! *(He places his arm with gun out the door.)* I got one of you, coppers! Who wants it next?

  [DAN *moves fast now, all the way across the room, driving his shoulder with full force into* ROBISH'S *back, catapulting him out the front door.* ROBISH'S *gun fires again with the impact. This brings* ELEANOR, *heedless now, out of the room, down the steps, as* DAN *slams door, locks it.* ELEANOR *runs to him.*

ELEANOR
  Dan, Dan, Dan . . .

  [DAN *turns, grabs Eleanor, swings her into the up Right corner of the room, out of line of the front door. He holds her there. A slight pause. Then* RALPHIE, *in bedroom, starts toward the bedroom door, which* ELEANOR *has left open; at this moment* GLENN, *in hall, stands up, groggily, holding his head, the gun still in his hand; he moves toward* RALPHIE, *who backs into bedroom as* GLENN *moves in on him, slowly as*

(BLACKOUT)

THE WALLINGS' ATTIC

BARD *is kneeling in the window with the rifle pointed out, looking through the telescopic sight.* CARSON *is behind him, with binoculars.*

BARD

It's Robish . . .

CARSON

Get him, Jesse. I'll give the signal to close in.

BARD *(lowering the rifle)*

Somebody pushed him out that door.

CARSON

He's heading for the car. Get him, Jesse!

BARD

Five minutes, Carson. Give Hilliard five more minutes!

CARSON

Hilliard might be dead!

BARD

Harry, I'm pleading with you. *Somebody shoved that big guy out the door. Five minutes!*

[*Slight pause.* CARSON *turns, crosses, switches on radio picks up mike.*

CARSON

All right, Jess. *(Into mike.)* Fredericks . . . Robish is in the Hilliard car. He's armed. Stop him.

[BARD *picks up the PA mike and speaks into it.*

BARD *(his voice sounding in distance over PA)*

Hilliard. Do you need us? *Hilliard.*

(BLACKOUT)

HILLIARD HOME

Outside, the floodlights remain on. GLENN, *still groggy from the blow, is in bedroom, gun on* RALPHIE, *who is on the bed, staring in terror at gun. In the living room,* DAN *and* ELEANOR *are helping* CHUCK *toward front door; he cannot stand without support.*

BARD'S VOICE *(the hollow sound of PA system)*
 Hilliard, can you hear me?

DAN
 Get him out of here!

 [DAN *unlocks and opens front door.*

CHUCK
 I flubbed it, didn't I?

DAN *(stepping out, waves off)*
 Hold fire out there!

RALPHIE *(in bedroom—as* GLENN *grabs him and holds him in front of himself as a shield)*
 Dad! Dad!

DAN *(as he and* ELEANOR *get* CHUCK *to door)*
 Get this boy some help.

CHUCK *(faintly)*
 I . . . I couldn't do anything else, I . . .

DAN *(taking the pistol from his hand)*
 You won't need this, son.

ELEANOR *(urgently, as she goes out with* CHUCK)
 Ralphie?

DAN *(firmly)*
 Ralphie's all right!

[ELEANOR *and* CHUCK *go out door.* DAN *turns, looking at pistol he has taken from* CHUCK. *He leaves the front door open wide.*

GLENN *(calling)*
I'm with him, Hilliard.

RALPHIE
Dad . . . are you coming?

DAN *(puts pistol in his pocket, turns to steps; speaks with grim determination—and on a note of triumph)*
I'm coming, son!

GLENN
In here, Hilliard. *(As* DAN *enters bedroom.)* I'm still gonna make it . . . still gonna pull it off. *(As* DAN *stops.)* You're gonna get me outta this.

DAN *(firmly, tonelessly)*
Let go of the boy, Griffin.

GLENN
Fat chance, them coppers out there!

BARD'S VOICE *(over PA)*
Griffin . . . Come out with your hands up . . . No gun!

[DAN *steps to window, opens it, calls out.*

DAN
Stay out of here. Turn off the light! *(The floodlights go out.* DAN *turns to Glenn.)* Now. Take your hands off him.

[GLENN *does so, but places the gun at back of Ralphie's neck.*

GLENN
You move, kid, I'll blow your head off.

DAN *(gently, urgently)*
Ralph . . . listen to me. That man is not going to hurt you.

GLENN
  Try budgin', kid, you'll find out.

DAN
  He's not going to hurt you at all because . . .

GLENN
  Lay off, my head's bustin', Hank's waitin', lay off . . .

DAN
  Ralph . . . have I ever lied to you?

  [RALPHIE *shakes his head.*

GLENN *(gun against* RALPHIE'S *neck)*
  Feel that? . . .

DAN *(To Ralphie)*
  Now—I want you to do exactly as I tell you. Because
  that gun is not loaded.

GLENN
  Stop bluffin', Hilliard, and let's get . . .

DAN
  It has no bullets in it, Ralph. Do you understand that?

  [RALPHIE *nods.*

GLENN
  You're lyin'! You wouldn't've brung it in here if . . .

DAN *(stepping back slightly, into hall, to clear the way)*
  Run!

  [*Without hesitation now,* RALPHIE *obeys. He runs, out
  bedroom door, past Dan, down the steps, out the front
  door.* GLENN *pulls the trigger of revolver. There is a click.*
  GLENN *is astonished. He steps to bedroom door and aims
  at Ralphie's back and clicks the gun, again and again,
  while a dazed, bleak horror mounts his face. Then his
  eyes meet* DAN'S *and he raises the gun as a weapon and*

steps toward Dan in hall—as DAN *brings out Chuck's gun and holds it pointed at Glenn. In background, during the pause, the sound of an ambulance siren starting up and pulling away.*

GLENN *(as he starts to strike Dan)*

You goddam . . . *(He breaks off, staring at the pistol in* DAN'S *hand, incredulous.)*

[*Long pause.*

DAN

Why don't you say something, Griffin? Clickety-clickety-click. *(Steps closer.)* You're not talking. Where's your voice now? *Call me Pop. Say* something, *damn you!*

GLENN

It ain't gonna be like this . . . Hank's waitin' . . .

DAN *(almost brutally)*

Griffin . . . your brother's not waiting anywhere. He's dead! *(*GLENN *is glassy-eyed, stunned.)* Full of police bullets. *Dead!*

GLENN *(suddenly wild)*

You're lyin', I don't believe . . . you're lyin'!!

DAN

You did that, too, damn you . . . *Damn you!*

[*The life goes out of* GLENN. *He swings full circle now . . . back to the stunned, depressed, lifeless phase of earlier in the evening. Despair . . . and worse. From now on he has no desire to survive. What follows is the death-wish all the way . . . finally erupting in his attempt to goad Dan into killing.*

DAN

It's your turn, Griffin . . . how do you like it?

GLENN *(bleakly)*

Go ahead . . . *(Lifelessly.)* Get it over with . . .

DAN

You don't like waiting? I've waited for hours . . . **all** of us . . . like years . . . all night . . . two days . . .

GLENN

Get it over with! *(He senses the hesitation in DAN, changes his tactics shrewdly.)* You ain't got it in you!

DAN *(low, hard)*

I've got it in me. *You* put it there!

GLENN *(goading)*

Then go ahead!

BARD'S VOICE *(on the PA)*

Hilliard, can you hear me? . . . Your wife's here. **And** the boy. They're both safe!

[*Pause.* GLENN *and* DAN *are both staring.*

GLENN

You ain't got it in you!

[DAN *tenses with the revolver pointed at Glenn. Then, suddenly realizing what he has almost done, he slowly lowers the gun, relieved.*

DAN *(quietly)*

You're right. *(Low—with disgust.)* Thank God, you're right! *(Quietly—with great dignity.)* Get out of my house. *(Then he steps to* GLENN *and slaps him a resounding, violent blow across the face.)* Get out of my house!

GLENN *(his voice whining . . . self-pity . . . a boy again)*

I'm gettin' out, Pop . . . I'm goin'. Only I'm takin' Hank along. You hit me for the last goddam time . . . You ain't ever gonna hit Hank or me again. *(He moves down the steps.)* I'm takin' Hank along **and you ain't** gonna see either one of us ever again! *(He crosses to front door.)* You can sit here'n rot in your stinkin' house, Mister God! I hated this crummy joint the day I was born!

DAN *(in amazement; weary disgust)*
Get out.

GLENN
You ain't gonna beat it into Hank'n me! Hank'n me's gonna be right on top! (GLENN, *now at front door, pauses, looks around, still dazed.* DAN *follows him down the steps.* GLENN *turns toward the open door, beckoning to an imaginary Hank.)* C'mon, Hank . . . we'll show 'em! *(The floodlights come on outside as* GLENN *steps in the doorway brandishing the gun. He goes out of sight, across porch, shouting.)* We'll show 'em, Hank, we'll show 'em, Hank, we . . .

[*A rifle shot is heard echoing down the quiet street.* DAN *stands quietly on the stairs . . . Lights remain on in Hilliard home through the following. Traveler does* not *close out view of Hilliard home.)*

THE WALLINGS' ATTIC

Lights rise on the attic. BARD *is lowering the rifle. He looks at* CARSON *a moment, a strange expression on his face.*

CARSON *(almost reassuringly)*
He asked for it, Jess. He . . . he acted like he was begging for it.

[BARD *looks at the rifle, then places it against the wall; slowly crosses to sit on trunk.*

CARSON *(moves Center to face Bard)*
You going over there?

BARD *(softly)*
  In a little while.

CARSON
  You feel all right, Jess?

BARD
  Just . . . maybe a little disgusted with the human race.

CARSON
  Mmmm. Including Hilliard?

BARD *(looks up at him, smiles wanly)*
  Thanks, Harry . . . No, *not* including Hilliard.

CARSON
  World's full of Hilliards.

  [CARSON *turns and goes out.* BARD *sits quietly, thinking
  . . . with his back to audience . . . as the lights fade
  slowly on the attic scene.*

  [*In the Hilliard home,* DAN *still stands unmoving on the
  steps, the gun in his limp hand, his head down.* ELEANOR
  *appears at front door; she looks stunned, worn. She gazes
  at the havoc that was her home. She moves slowly to the
  sofa, almost helplessly rearranges a pillow.* RALPHIE *enters
  behind her; he crosses to* DAN, *whose head is down;*
  RALPHIE *stands gazing at his father . . .*

  [*As* CINDY *enters the living room from dining room,* DAN
  *lifts his head, looks at her; then slowly, he turns his gaze
  on* ELEANOR. *Their eyes meet, hold. They stand looking
  at each other as though cognizant of the miracle . . . as
  though seeing in each other, and perhaps in the world,
  more than words could convey.*

(DIMOUT)

SLOW CURTAIN

THE DESPERATE HOURS

PROPERTY PLOT

ACT ONE—Scene I

Sheriff's Office

Wall clock (rear wall)
Desk and swivel chair (down Right)
Metal files (rear wall)
Radio and intercom apparatus (on desk)
Papers (on desk)
Telephone (on desk)
Gun (Bard)
Clothing rack (at Left)
Teletype message (Winston)
Cigarettes (Carson)

Scene II

Hilliard Home

Milk in glass (Ralphie)
Pad and pencil (Eleanor)
Indianapolis Star (on porch)
2 phones
Cup of coffee (Dan)
Football (on sofa)
Glass of orange juice (Cindy)
Auto horn
Portable radio (end table Center)
Revolver (Glenn)
Clothes (bedroom)
Keys (dining room)
Purse (on sofa)
Locket (in purse)
Money (in purse)
Automatic (in closet)

Humidor (end table)
Cigars (humidor)
Cigarettes (coffee table)
Lighter (coffee table)

Scene IV

Hilliard Home
Carton of cigarettes (end table)
Box of cigars (end table Center)
Ashtrays (end and coffee tables)
Coffee cups (table and floor)
Food (on tables)
Key (in door Right)
Newspaper (Dan)
Sweater (Hank)
Radio (Hank)

Scene VI

Hilliard Home
Cigar (Robish)
Wrist-watch (Dan)

Scene VII

Sheriff's Office
Deck of cards (desk)

Scene VIII

Hilliard Home
Key (front door)
Whiskey bottle (Dan)
Gun (Hank)
Keys (Cindy)

ACT TWO—Scene I

Sheriff's Office
Playing cards (Carson)
Reports (desk)

Scene II

Hilliard Home
Towels
Road map (on chair)

Scene IV

Hilliard Home
Cigarette (Hank)
Newspaper (on porch)
Checkbook (Eleanor)
Pen (Eleanor)
Billfold (Patterson)

Scene V

Sheriff's Office
Large manilla envelope (Carson)
Check (envelope)
17 dollar bills (envelope)
Ball-point pen (envelope)
Snuffbox (envelope)
Wallet (envelope)
Driver's license (envelope)
Photograph (envelope)

Scene VI

Hilliard Home
Bottle (on sofa)
Composition book (Ralphie)

Scene VII

Sheriff's Office
Map of Indianapolis (back wall, Left)
Letter (Carson)

Scene VIII

Hilliard Home
Automatic (Hank)

Composition book (on sofa)

Scene IX

Sheriff's Office
Driver's license (Bard)
Revolver (on desk)
Newspaper (on desk)
List on desk)
Letter (on desk)
Rifle (Winston)

ACT THREE—Scene II

Walling Attic
Iron bed frame
Boxes
Radio
Trunks
Binoculars
Rifle

Scene III

Hilliard Home
Portable radio (on table)

Scene IV

Walling Attic
Binoculars (Bard)
Letter (Bard)
Special delivery letter (Dan)
Money (in envelope)
Bullets (in revolver)

Scene V

Hilliard Home
Revolvers (Dan, Robish, Glenn)
Envelope (Dan)
Money (in envelope)

Scene VI

Walling Attic
Binoculars (Carson)

Scene VII

Hilliard Home
Revolver (Chuck)

Scene VIII

Walling Attic
Rifle (Bard)

Scene IX

Revolver (Dan)

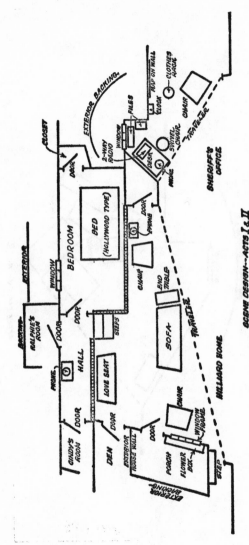

SCENE DESIGN—ACTS I & II

"THE DESPERATE HOURS"

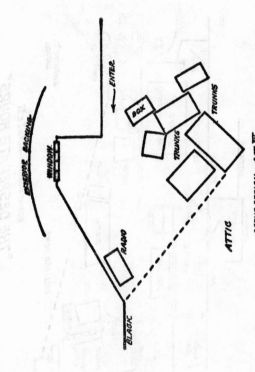

THE HILLIARD'S HOUSE

EXTERIOR BACKING

WINDOW

ENTER

BOX

TRUNKS

TRUNKS

RADIO

BLACK

ATTIC

SCENE DESIGN -- ACT III

"THE DESPERATE HOURS"

TAKE HER, SHE'S MINE

By PHOEBE and HENRY EPHRON

COMEDY—2 ACTS

11 men, 6 women—Various sets

Art Carney and Phyllis Thaxter played the Broadway roles of parents of two typically American girls enroute to college. The phases of a girl's life are cause for rich enjoyment—except to fearful fathers. Through the first two years, the authors tell us, college girls are frightfully sophisticated about all departments of human life. Then they pass into the "liberal" period of causes and humanitarianism, and some into the intellectual lethargy of beatniksville. Finally, they start to think seriously of life and marriage to come. There are rippling scenes of ogling students from the nearby male schools, of jibberish verse and folk-singing, and of the devious habits of American dating. It's an experience in growing up, as much for the parents as for the girls. "A warming comedy. A delightful play about parents vs. kids. It's loaded with laughs. It's going to be a smash hit."—*N. Y. Times.*

(Royalty, $50-$25.)

ENTER LAUGHING

By JOSEPH STEIN

adapted from the novel by Carl Reiner

FARCE—2 ACTS

7 men, 4 women. A stage, wagons, and insets

"Let's not waste time on ifs, buts and maybes. 'Enter Laughing' is marvelously funny." Thus did the *Times* critic begin his review of this unheralded "sleeper" that convulsed Broadway audiences for a whole season, with the help of Alan Arkin, Vivian Blaine, Sylvia Sidney and Alan Mowbrey. It is the account of the riotous sojourn of a stage-struck youth who works as the delivery boy in a sewing machine factory. His parents want him to be a druggist; but as soon as he has saved enough money he enlists in a hammy, semi-professional company that will put anybody in any play for the right amount. However, he is, as the *Daily News* critic reported, "a terrible, dreadful actor, and the scene of his first performance is joyously funny. It takes a good actor to act like a bad actor." He proceeds to splash through romantic scenes with the ham manager's daughter, with another fellow's date, and finally with the office girl who was meant for him all the time.

(Slightly restricted. Royalty, $50-$25, where available.)

THE TRAITOR

Melodrama. 2 acts. By Herman Wouk. 15 men, 3 women. Interior. Modern costumes.

This exciting and intelligent melodrama with Lee Tracy in the leading role opened to thunderous acclaim at the Forty-eighth Street Theatre, New York. The title figure of *The Traitor* is a thoughtful and earnest atomic scientist who has no regard for communism, but who sincerely believes that the only way to prevent the catastrophe of a final world war is to surrender the secret of the atomic bomb to Russia. As he reasons, the sharing of an open secret would bring an end to hysteria and arms races. His fiancee receives in his school study an old friend of hers, a Lieutenant in Naval Intelligence. He proceeds cautiously, gathering evidence. Then, in the scientist's absence, a naval crew suddenly descends upon the study to make a sweeping examination and to wire it for sound. This scene is a breath-taking moment that Broadway has never forgotten. It precipitates the crisis in which the scientist finally understands his treachery. He lends himself heroically in the gun-battle climax when a high-ranking Russian secret agent appears. "There is a sense of pulsing melodrama in town in *The Traitor*, as hot as tomorrow's newspaper."—*N. Y. World Telegram.*

(Royalty, $50.00.)

DARKNESS AT NOON

Tragedy. 3 acts. By Sidney Kingsley, based on the novel by Arthur Koestler. 18 men, 3 women. Interior. Modern and military costumes.

This play, winner of the Drama Critics Award, starred Claude Rains in the Playwrights Company production at the Alvin Theatre. It is the story of a Soviet Commissar with considerable power in the party who is jailed as the curtain goes up. He has made two serious errors from the viewpoint of his superiors: he once fell in love with his secretary, and he shot off his mouth at an inopportune moment. The three acts of the play detail his torment and frustration in the cell, a situation dramatically heightened by the ability of the other prisoners to communicate with him through a system of tapping on the walls, plus the retrospective scenes which explain his sentence and the series of ludicrously unjust hearings leading to his execution. "Brilliant anti-Communist propaganda."—*Herald-Tribune.* "Deeply and hauntingly impressive." —*Post.* "Pungent, spectacular melodrama on a political theme."—*Times.* "The only contemporary and contemporarily important drama we have on the stage."—*Daily News.*

(Royalty, $50.00.)

Come Blow Your Horn
By NEIL SIMON

COMEDY
3 men, 4 women—Interior

This fresh and delightful comedy was the surprise hit of the recent New York season. Harry Baker, owner of the largest artificial fruit business in the east, is the father of two sons. One is a 33-year old playboy; the other a different, 21-year-old with an urge to assert himself. These two are continually trying their father's easily abused patience. Alan works only two days a week and goes on skiing or golfing jaunts with attractive female companions the other five. Buddy, hitherto an obedient son who even kissed Aunt Gussie through her veil at Dad's request, has moved into Alan's apartment, leaving a rebellious letter by way of explanation. The richly comic complications that ensue are unfailingly inventive and arise out of character, are never mere gags. "A slick, lively, funny comedy."—*N. Y. Times.* "It's completely nuts and banging with laughs."—*N. Y. World-Telegram & Sun.* "Warm hearted and amusing."—*N. Y. Daily News.*

(Royalty, $50-$25.)

A Thousand Clowns
By HERB GARDNER

COMEDY
4 men, 1 woman, 1 boy 12 years old—2 interiors

Having created America's funniest creatures, the Nebishes, Herb Gardner turned his sights on Broadway and created the funniest play of the season, with "A Thousand Clowns." Jason Robards, Jr., opened in the role of a bachelor uncle who had been left to rear his precocious nephew. He has tired of writing cheap comedy for a children's television program, and now finds himself unemployed. But he also finds he has the free time to saunter through New York and do everything he has always wanted—like standing on Park Avenue in the dawn's early light and hollering, "All right, all you rich people: everybody out in the street for volleyball." This is not the right upbringing for a boy, however, and so a social service team comes to investigate him. Soon, however, he is solving their problems for them. Then he has to go back to work, or lose his nephew. Then on the other hand, he might even marry the girl social worker. The only thing we're certain of is that he will always be a cheerful non-conformist of the first rank.

(Slightly restricted. Royalty, $50-$25, where available.)

DON'T DRINK THE WATER

By WOODY ALLEN

FARCE

12 men, 4 women—Interior

A CASCADE OF COMEDY FROM ONE OF OUR FUNNIEST CO-
MEDIANS, and a solid hit on Broadway, this affair takes place inside
an American embassy behind the Iron Curtain. An American tourist, caterer by trade, and his family of wife and daughter rush into the embassy
two steps ahead of the police, who suspect them of spying and picture-
taking. But it's not much of a refuge, for the ambassador is absent and
his son, now in charge, has been expelled from a dozen countries and the
whole continent of Africa. Nevertheless, they carefully and frantically plot
their escape, and the ambassador's son and the caterer's daughter even
have time to fall in love. "Because Mr. Allen is a working comedian himself, a number of the lines are perfectly agreeable . . . and there's quite
a delectable bit of business laid out by the author and manically elab-
orated by the actor. . . . The gag is pleasantly outrageous and impeccably
performed."—*N. Y. Times.* "Moved the audience to great laughter. . . .
Allen's imagination is daffy, his sense of the ridiculous is keen and gags
snap, crackle and pop."—*N. Y. Daily News.* "It's filled with funny lines
. . . A master of bright and hilarious dialogue."—*N. Y. Post.*

(Slightly restricted. Royalty, $50-$25, where available.)

THE ODD COUPLE

By NEIL SIMON

COMEDY

6 men, 2 women—Interior

NEIL SIMON'S THIRD SUCCESS in a row begins with a group of the
boys assembled for cards in the apartment of a divorced fellow, and if
the mess of the place is any indication, it's no wonder that his wife left
him. Late to arrive is another fellow who, they learn, has just been separated from his wife. Since he is very meticulous and tense, they fear
he might commit suicide, and so go about locking all the windows. When
he arrives, he is scarcely allowed to go to the bathroom alone. As life
would have it, the slob bachelor and the meticulous fellow decide to bunk
together—with hilarious results. The patterns of their own disastrous mar-
riages begin to reappear in this arrangement; and so this too must end.
"The richest comedy Simon has written and purest gold for any theatre-
goer. . . . This glorious play."—*N. Y. World-Telegram & Sun.* "His skill
is not only great but constantly growing. . . . There is scarcely a moment
that is not hilarious."—*N. Y. Times.*

(Royalty, $50-$35.)

A RAISIN IN THE SUN

By LORRAINE HANSBERRY

DRAMA

7 men, 3 women, 1 child—Interior

A Negro family is cramped in a flat on the south side of Chicago. They are a widow, her son (a chauffeur), his wife, his sister, and his little boy. The widow is expecting a $10,000 insurance settlement on her husband's death, and her son is constantly begging her to give him the money so that he can become co-owner of a liquor store. He wants to quit chauffeuring, to become a business man, and to be able to leave his son a little bit more than his own father, a brick-layer, had left him: this is the only way a Negro can continue to improve his lot. The widow, meantime, has placed a down-payment on a house where they can have sunlight, and be rid of roaches. The despair of the young husband is intense. His mother reluctantly turns over the remaining $6500 to him, as head of the house. He invests in the liquor store, his partner absconds, and his dream is forever dead. A representative from the better (white) neighborhood, into which they planned to move, calls on them and offers to reimburse them handsomely for their investment. But our young man now real-izes that a little bit of dignity is all he can ever count on, and he plans to move his family to the new house.

(Royalty, $50-$25.)

PURLIE VICTORIOUS

By OSSIE DAVIS

COMEDY

6 men, 3 women—Exterior, 2 comp.

By taking all the cliches of plays, about the lovable old south and the love that existed between white masters and colored slaves, Ossie Davis has compounded a constantly comic play. Purlie Victorious has come back to his shabby cabin to announce that he will reacquire the local church and ring the freedom bell. There is an inheritance due to a colored cousin, which would be sufficient to buy the church, but unfortunately it also is controlled by the white-head plantation colonel. Purlie Victorious tries to send a newcomer to the colonel to impersonate the heiress, not only is she found out, but the colonel makes a pass at her. Eventually the church is recovered, services are again held in it, and the freedom bell rings. It is the dialogue, though, that makes the events so uproarious ("Are you trying to get non-violent with me, boy?") or human ("Oh, child, being colored can be a lot of fun when they ain't nobody looking"). There's uncommonly good sense in such a line as the one delivered to Purlie when he was about to beat the colonel with the colonel's well-worn bullwhip: "You can't do wrong just because it's right."

(Royalty, $50-$25.)

NEW
Plays

ALL OVER
ALL THE GIRLS CAME OUT TO PLAY
BUTLEY
FOUR IN A GARDEN
LAST OF THE RED HOT LOVERS
MAD SHOW
PRISONER OF SECOND AVENUE
PROMENADE, ALL!
REAL INSPECTOR HOUND
6 RMS RIV VU
SLEUTH
STICKS AND BONES
VIVAT, VIVAT REGINA!
WHEN DID YOU LAST SEE MY MOTHER

Availability Information on Request